FROSTED PLUM FEARS

CLAIRE'S CANDLES

BOOK NINE

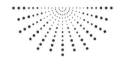

AGATHA FROST

PINK TREE PUBLISHING

WANT TO BE KEPT UP TO DATE WITH AGATHA
FROST RELEASES? *SIGN UP THE FREE NEWSLETTER!*

www.AgathaFrost.com

You can also follow **Agatha Frost** across social media.
Search 'Agatha Frost' on:

Facebook
Twitter
Goodreads
Instagram

ALSO BY AGATHA FROST

1. Pancakes and Corpses

Other

The Agatha Frost Winter Anthology

Peridale Cafe Book 1-10

Peridale Cafe Book 11-20

Claire's Candles Book 1-3

CHAPTER ONE

*S*ugar and spice, and all things nice.

The delicious scents of the Christmas market would make the perfect festive candle, thought Claire Harris, as she weaved between the stalls under a blanket of twinkling lights. Tugging her wool scarf tighter, she peered into the rattling box of glass candle jars and made a mental note to attempt to bottle the scent of the market.

The market-inspired candle would have to wait until next Christmas.

This year, she'd built her winter range around her new star product, the frosted plum candle. She could smell it even through the sealed lids. Spiced citrus sat atop a rich and tangy plum middle mixed with a dash of grounding vanilla, lying on a deep amber musk bed. It wasn't one of her usual festive scents, but it had turned out to be rather irresistible to all who popped the lid for a whiff.

Up ahead, Claire spotted her Claire's Candles stall sandwiched between the clock tower and The Hesketh Arms, a prime spot she'd reserved months ago when she'd first heard the market was coming to Northash. Her father, Alan Harris, entertained the customers with his jolly conversation; Claire's mother, Janet, said he could talk to anyone about anything until the cows came home. Claire's friend, Em, the local yoga instructor, worked alongside him, wrapping jars and wax melts in the brown paper bags. Above them, a hand-painted sign—made with the help of Claire's boyfriend, Ryan, and his kids—read 'Claire's Candles: Presents That Light Up Christmas!'

"Hard at work or hardly working?" Claire laughed, setting down the heavy box packed with candles. "Christmas Eve's Eve is one of the busiest days of the year for my second Christmas in the shop."

"Can barely keep these plum candles on the stall," Alan said, plucking out jars to fill up the diminishing frosted plum row at the front. "You've come up with another winner, little one."

"Thank the last-minute shoppers."

"And the ravages of capitalism," Em said with a jolly smile, handing a bag across the stall to a little old lady peeping through a scarf longer than she was tall. "Though

I like how this time of year puts everyone in a good mood. And your dad is right. This new candle is a one-whiff wonder."

Claire scanned the market and caught glimpses of her flame logo emblazoned on brown paper bags hanging from the crooks of shoppers' arms.

"Tomorrow's 'Largest Plum Pudding in Northash' record attempt isn't hurting," Claire said, glancing at the large white tent dominating the market on the other side of the clock tower. "That new chef from The Park Inn has created plum pudding pandemonium, and the shop's takings are grateful."

"Think he'll break the record?" Em asked.

"That Marco's got magic hands," her father said, rubbing his gloves together after twisting the last plum jar so the foil label faced out just so. "The Park Inn will never hold a candle to The Hesketh, but the duck confit I had with your mother the other night was superb. You'd barely know it was the same pub."

Her gaze drifted over the glowing windows of The Hesketh Arms. Through the frost-lined glass, she saw Malcolm and Theresa huddled together, their heads lowered in tense whispers. As Marco—handsome enough to be a model with thick oiled hair and stylish stubble—emerged from the event tent, Claire noticed Malcolm shoot the chef a seething glare before turning his back. Claire's brows creased, a question forming in her mind.

Were they resentful of the competition from The Park Inn's new upscale menu?

"He's got most of the village under his spell," Em whispered, plucking a thick wad of notes from the takings box to stuff in Claire's pocket. "Half of my yoga clients walk out of the gym and go straight to The Park Inn these days. He even has gourmet vegan options, not that I've tried them at those prices."

"I *will* pay you for helping me with my stall."

"And I *won't* accept." Em winked, tugging her woolly hat tighter over her buzzed-to-the-scalp hair. "Beats sitting on my narrowboat in this weather."

"I can't believe old Victor Michaels' record might finally be broken after all these years," her father thought aloud, his faraway gaze looking at the tent. "I remember taking you and your mum to watch the grand unveiling, little one. You'd have only been a toddler, but given how huge your eyes were, even you knew you were witnessing history." He chuckled. "Tasted amazing, too."

"Maybe that's where it all went wrong," Claire said, patting her rounded waistline. "Chefs like Marco don't turn up in Northash often. Or ever, for that matter. Makes a difference from the usual microwave slop they used to serve at The Park Inn." Leaning into her father's ear, poking out of his bobble hat, she whispered, "Damon and I are putting twenty quid on him beating the record at the bookies if you want in?"

"Twenty?" He nibbled his lip as he dug in his pocket. "Would need to be a full tonne to beat Victor's record." He stuffed the shiny purple note into Claire's hand and added, "Don't tell your mother."

"What did Victor's plum pudding weigh?"

"Think Victor was aiming for the full tonne," he said, nodding to someone he knew across the market, "but he was a few pounds shy. Not that he had a record to beat. He *set* the record, but I'll never forget how furious Victor was—he claimed the alcohol to set the thing on fire burned away the extra two pounds to round it up. Came in at nine-hundred-and-ninety-eight pounds."

"I'm sure that's what the scale will say come January if I keep scoffing mince pies like I have."

"Always welcome to join my yoga classes at the gym," Em offered. "There's a 'Same Year, New Me' deal to get people in before the inevitable New Year rush."

Promising that she'd think about it—and knowing she'd likely skip signing up for a dreaded gym membership for another year—Claire gathered up the empty boxes and returned to add the morning's takings to her shop's till. She rounded the clock tower, passing the large event tent that housed the pop-up kitchen for the plum pudding attempt. Marco and his team had taken over the space days ago, shrouding their record-seeking attempt in secrecy.

As Claire hurried past, the flap of the white marquee

was open just enough for her to glimpse the expansive prep space inside. She paused, the temptation to spy too strong to resist. Within, Marco's sous-chef, Grant Parker, had his back to her at a central island filled with industrial sacks of sugar. His shoulders hunched as he leaned over an array of gleaming knives in a wooden block, his movements stiff and tense. Claire knew Grant only by his fiery reputation from The Park Inn.

Grant swivelled his head from side to side, his gaze sweeping the area. He pivoted towards the tent entrance, and Claire's heart wobbled as she darted out of view, barely avoiding his line of sight. She heard his aggressive bark from her hiding spot. "Can I *help* you?"

"Just passing!" Claire called out, quickening her pace as she backed away.

While Marco garnered near universal affection from locals for his Park Inn overhaul, his second-in-command proved a disruptive presence. Claire had thought the villagers had mangled Grant's reputation, but she'd heard his ranting and raving blaring from the kitchen during her only visit to try out the new menu at the village's 'other' pub.

Leaving the tent, she squeezed through the edge of the market and emerged in front of her candle shop. A group of shoppers crowded around the new plum-themed window display as she pushed through the door, rattling the bell.

Ryan Tyler, spun around alongside his kids, eleven-year-old Amelia and eight-year-old Hugo, inspecting the display of hand-painted Christmas cards. Her cheeks flushed at the sight of her boyfriend with his children.

"You're back," Amelia said, her face lighting up. "Hugo said you'd been chopped up and put in the plum pudding."

"That's what *you* said."

"No, I didn't." Amelia shrugged, turning back to the cards. "These are well good, Dad."

"Nice to see you both, too," Claire said, ruffling their hair—sandy tinged with red, the same as Ryan's—as she joined them at the cards. "Your dad did a cracking job painting these cards, don't you think?"

"Cracking?" Amelia arched a brow, half-rolling her eyes. "None of the candles he painted are cracked. Old people..."

A thirty-seven, Claire resented the 'old' label, but she let it slide.

"They're perfect, Dad," Hugo muttered, plucking the edges of the card depicting gingerbread people crowding around a large candle like they were worshipping it. "I helped fold these."

"That's why they're *all* so wonky," Amelia said. "My Christmas tree ones are better."

"They're all folded perfectly," Ryan cut in. He straightened the cards, fixing Claire with his charming, dimpled smile that still made her stomach flip, even after all these years of knowing him. "Sorry, I didn't mean to ambush your shop. They wanted to see if there were any left. Still quite a lot."

"Two shopping days left until Christmas," she pointed out, glancing at the clock. "Okay, so one and a half days."

Claire saw the worry in Ryan's apple-green eyes as he pushed his smile wider. She'd held an unrequited torch for Ryan Tyler—her childhood cul-de-sac neighbour—for most of her life. She still had to pinch herself that they were about to spend their second Christmas as an official couple together, though this was the first Christmas she'd convinced him to paint her a range of cards for her shop. She'd have hoped they'd all sold by now and had promised as much, but the racks were still stuffed. Regardless, she wished Ryan believed in his artistic talents as much as she did.

"I'll knock ten percent off when the sale starts on Boxing Day," she assured him, squeezing his hand. "They'll fly off the shelves for the people who like to get ahead for next—"

A sudden market-silencing commotion outside disrupted her, and the kids ran up to the window. They pressed their noses against the glass on either side of the giant papier mâché sparkling plum that kept drawing the crowds to take pictures.

Letting go of Ryan's hand, Claire joined them at the

window overlooking the square, looking in the same direction everyone outside faced—the giant white tent. Grant Parker's distinctive gruff tones bellowed from inside like an afternoon in The Park Inn. Claire was about to joke about him having seen one too many episodes of Gordon Ramsey's *Kitchen Nightmares* when the tent's flap flung open, and Grant Parker stormed out, face crimson with rage. He tore the tall white chef's hat from his bald head and tossed it into a nearby bin.

Marco appeared at the tent's entrance, his usually cheerful face twisting into a disappointed frown as he stroked at his black stubble. He shook his head in Grant's direction before disappearing into the event tent, barking orders at whoever had joined the tent since Claire had peeped at Grant near the knives.

"What was that about?" Ryan wondered as he came up behind Claire, slipping his arm around her waist.

"Not sure, but I saw Grant acting oddly when I passed by earlier." She turned into Ryan's firm embrace. "Seems like he can't keep a lid on his temper."

"That sous-chef comes to my boxercise classes at the gym and punches like his life depends on it," Ryan said as the market bustle resumed outside. "He acts like he doesn't know the whole village is watching him."

"I'm sure the drama drives more people to The Park Inn. Seems like theatre, but what we just saw..." Claire sighed, glancing back at the white tent. "Doesn't matter.

Give me the quiet home cooking at The Hesketh Arms any day of the week."

Over Ryan's shoulder, Claire's best friend—and only employee at the shop—Damon Gilbert, strolled in from the storeroom. He clutched a box with frosted plum candles under his arm, holding a *Doctor Who* graphic novel in the other. He glanced up with a frown. "What did I miss?"

"A lot of nothing," Claire said, joining him to restock the central Star Candle of the Month display as more customers came in. "And reading comics on the job? I could fire you for that."

"Before Christmas?" Damon muttered, pulling the book closer to his nose. "Sally might like that. She keeps saying two words that make me feel sick." Peering over the book, he whispered. "*Skiing holiday.*"

Claire laughed, and as Ryan ferried the kids through the door with a wave before it shut, she decided to push aside her concerns about the plum pudding drama.

Like she'd told Damon, a lot of nothing.

Probably.

CHAPTER TWO

*N*estled on her shop's doorstep on Christmas Eve, Claire cradled her hot morning coffee, savouring the later opening hour. Christmas Eve had transformed Northash's square into a scene from a vintage postcard, a joyful yuletide buzz in the early morning air—the mood would turn sour when the shopping hours dwindled as the Big Day drew closer. For now, Claire was content to sit, sip, and watch the morning go by.

Unfolding the *Northash Observer*, a bold headline announced the plum pudding record attempt that had been stirring the village into a frenzy. The article highlighted Chef Marco's ambition to surpass Victor Michaels' legendary feat: a nearly thousand-pound pudding, a culinary marvel crafted over thirty years ago.

Despite Victor's achievement, the enormous plum pudding record paled in comparison to his impressive lion's mane of thick auburn hair.

With a sip of her hot coffee, Claire's smile grew. It must have been a slow news day. The record attempt was so silly that it turned back into being charming. She pictured herself tucking into the huge pudding later that afternoon, regardless of whether Marco beat the record. The history books were one thing, but how would it taste?

Slurping the last few drops from the plastic lid, Claire pushed herself off the step, ready for the day ahead. She'd given Damon the day off, leaving her alone to battle the shoppers. She held out the newspaper to a passing woman who'd been craning her neck to look at the headline, and as the woman thanked her and hurried off, Claire scanned the busy market square. She hoped the charming silliness of the plum pudding party would keep the air light, but if she knew the villagers of Northash, she wouldn't be surprised if she'd be pulling apart two people fighting over the last frosted plum candle by closing.

The morning calm was pierced by a woman shrieking into her phone at one of the stalls facing the candle shop. Claire landed on a familiar figure across the road—Leslie Clark, former chef of The Park Inn, behind her cupcake stall.

Leslie's reputation in Northash had soured following her poor handling of being ousted in favour of Marco. Nobody had known Leslie's name, less a chef and more a 'microwave technician', until she'd threatened to 'ruin Marco' in the middle of the pub on the day the brewery gave her the boot.

Claire would have left her be, but she couldn't help but notice that Leslie's rant down the phone was punctuated with glares and tossed fingers towards Marco's tent. She crossed the road to throw her Marley's Café takeaway cup in the nearest bin, lingering by the hand-knitted hats and scarfs neighbouring the cupcakes. She smiled at the yawning stallholder, warming her hands up with her breath, but her ear was pointed in Leslie's direction.

"It's not *fair*!" she growled with a whine that sounded more like a fourteen-year-old than a nearly forty-something. "He waltzes in here with his fancy restaurant experience and gets handed everything on a platter. Nobody asked for fine dining at the pub until *he* showed up, and now *this*?"

Leslie stormed off towards the event tent with determined strides. Claire, sucked in by the spectacle—and never feeling more like her mother—followed across the cobbled square.

Peering through the same gap Claire had found herself in the day before, Leslie spied inside.

"Yeah, well, it's an unfair advantage..." Leslie muttered, her tone laced with bitterness. "I won't let him win. Don't you worry."

Claire edged closer, feigning interest in a nearby stall's handmade baubles, her ears straining to catch more. She smiled at the stallholder despite the tree decorations having some of the worst painting she'd seen and the steepest prices possible.

"If I beat his record, he wouldn't be laughing *then*, would he?" Leslie said after some silence. "Yes, I know it would be expensive. I... I don't know. I'd think of something, wouldn't I? It's *my* birthright, not his."

Claire's attention snagged on movement across the market as Leslie shouted into her phone. Malcolm, the pub landlord, stood outside The Hesketh Arms, phone clamped to his ear, face mottled, his free hand slicing through the air. His heated gestures reminded Claire of Leslie's venom towards Marco. She chewed her lip, wondering. Was Leslie on the phone with Malcolm, stirring up trouble? Without warning, Leslie turned from the tent, her eyes landing on Claire, who couldn't look away quickly enough.

Busted.

"Can I help you?" Leslie barked, scanning Claire up and down, echoing Grant's words from the day before. Her voice, once only heard shouting 'service' in a pleasant tone from The Park Inn's kitchen, now dripped with icy disdain. "*What*? Do you want to take a picture?"

"I was… looking…" Claire stammered, gesturing to the stall. She pulled out the twenty-pound note her father had given her for the bet and handed it over, plucking a red bauble with wobbly silver glitter lines. "Lovely."

When Claire turned with her purchase in a plain paper bag, Leslie had retreated to her cupcake stall, rigid and stalking Claire like a hawk. Moving onto the mulled wine stall nearest the white tent, Claire decided to avoid looking in Leslie's direction to starve her of ammunition for another outburst. Instead, she let the peek inside the tent beckon her once again.

The rich, intoxicating scents of simmering fruit and brandy shrouded her as she breathed deeply, transfixed by industrial mixers whirring and ovens glowing. The production set-up reminded her of the gigantic machines at the candle factory on the hill where she used to work. She wondered if her shop would now sell handmade baked goods instead of homemade candles if she'd worked in a factory that made plum puddings.

At the central gleaming island, Marco rifled through the box of knives.

"Has *anyone* seen the paring knife?" he called, leaning against the island and staring at the floor. No response came. "*Hello*? Anyone?"

"Not seen it, Chef," a young woman in chef's whites replied. "It's not like you to misplace anything, Chef."

"*I* didn't misplace it," Marco snapped, scanning the block again. "I want this kitchen searched inside out before we leave tonight, but it's not important right now." Rubbing the bridge of his nose, he exhaled. "*Why* can I hear *silence* when we have a tonne of plum pudding to make? We have a *record* to break."

The small army of white-clad helpers jumped back to work, and not wanting to risk being caught out for a third time, Claire pulled back from the peeping place and collided straight into someone.

"Sneaking around?" Damon laughed, steadying the pile of festive shopping bags he held. "How out of character, boss."

"Totally out of character," added Sally with a wink, Damon's girlfriend, and another of Claire's friends. "Shouldn't you be at the shop?"

"Late opening," Claire said, glancing over her shoulder at the tent one last time before drifting back into the market with Sally and Damon. "And I wasn't sneaking around, I was just… shouldn't you be at work too?"

"No one buys houses at Christmas," Sally said, arching a brow. "Smith and Smith have shut up shop until the New Year, speaking of which… thought about doing the same?"

Damon caught Claire's eye and gave her a subtle headshake.

"People might not buy houses, but they still buy candles. We were crammed the week between Christmas and New Year last year."

"*The Twilight Zone*, I call it. Nobody knows how to act, and everyone is just... waiting for New Year's." Sighing, Sally nudged Damon. "Because we thought we could head for the slopes for a few days. I haven't been skiing in years, and can you believe Damon has *never* been?"

Damon's cheeks prickled a deep maroon as he distracted himself with the sci-fi comic books stall at the end of the row.

"I cannot believe that," Claire said, deadpan. "But also... neither have I."

"Which is *why* I wanted you to close the shop. I thought you could bring Ryan, too. A little double date holiday?" Sally's giddiness only lasted until Claire didn't jump at the offer. "Since you're chained to your shop, maybe you could give Damon some last-minute holiday leave?"

Damon paled, his eyes finding Claire's with an unspoken plea, shaking his head with the slowness of someone being marched to death row. Sally glanced at him with an adoring smile; the headshaking stopped, and his eyes creased as he smiled back.

"I'm not sure I'd be able to leave Claire in the lurch

like that," Damon said in a small voice. "Not so last minute. Like Claire said, those post-Christmas sales are surprisingly busy."

"Oh, he's right," Claire agreed. "I'd be lost without my right hand. You know what my brain is like with numbers, Sal. Damon takes one day off, and everything goes sideways."

Sally nodded through her disappointment. Behind her back, Damon mouthed a subtle but emphatic 'Thank you!' as a long and deep sigh of relief escaped him like a deflating balloon.

"Well... maybe next year," Sally recovered brightly before giving Damon a swift peck on the cheek. "A double date holiday does sound fun, though. If not skiing, a cruise? Or a little cabin up in The Lakes?" Checking her watch, Sally's attention drifted. "I should get on with the Christmas shopping. I still haven't figured out what to buy my mother yet. I don't want her thinking I like her *too* much, but I also don't want to get written out of the will..."

As Damon's shoulders slumped with relief, Sally vanished into the thickening crowd.

"Saved by the candle shop," he said, patting her back. "Thanks for that, mate. I don't think I had the heart. You know what she's like when she gets an idea."

"I do. I'm surprised she didn't bring up the thought of me and Ryan getting a mortgage on a house together again." She tiptoed to watch Sally picking up the knitted hats at the stall next to the cupcakes; Leslie had stopped watching Claire and was back to staring at the tent. "She's right, though. I should get to the shop…"

"What's got you so distracted, Claire Marple?" Damon asked, rocking on his heels. "Anything to do with Grant storming out yesterday? You haven't been the same since."

"No," Claire said, and then she thought about it. "Maybe."

She hesitated before deciding to confide about the missing knife to her trusted friend. She recounted the odd tensions mounting around Marco's record attempt, from both Grant's and Leslie's unconcealed resentment to the unsettling disappearance of the blade from Marco's collection.

"Strange things are happening surrounding this plum pudding."

Damon crossed his arms, furrowing his brow as he listened intently. "You mean to tell me the fact it's going to weigh a literal tonne isn't strange enough?"

"*Stranger* things."

"Well, I say you get your head out of the upside down," Damon whispered, nodding at the shop. "Your giant plum has drawn quite the crowd already."

Claire looked off to her shop, where a small gathering waited for her to open the shop to buy their last-minute Secret Santa stocking stuffers and their 'What to buy the mother I secretly resent' scented candles.

"Enough about my giant plum," she said, batting his arm with the back of her hand. "I swear I'm going on a diet in January."

"You and me both." He patted his belly. "January... 2040?"

"Steady on. Why so soon?"

"Good point," he said, focusing on the comic book stall at the end of the row. "Do you mind if I..."

"Go browse till your heart's content," she said, shoving him. "It's your day off, and I should mind my own business. You're right. A giant plum pudding *is* strange enough."

Alone once more, Claire's smile faded as she walked back towards her shop. Despite her dismissal, there *was* a strange tension in the air, and she was sure she was the only one not connected to the event who'd picked up on it.

The force of someone's grip on her arm shocked Claire from her brooding before her foot left the curb. She turned, expecting to see the jolly face of Damon, or maybe even Sally asking for a rethink of the skiing holiday, but Leslie's snarled glare met her.

"Eavesdropping *again?*" Leslie barked, taking Claire in again. "I knew you were snooping before. What's your problem, *hmm*? Did Marco pay you off to make sure I behaved myself today?"

Claire recoiled, words escaping her as she looked down at the nails digging through her padded coat. A stunned hush rippled through curious onlookers nearby. Before Claire could defuse the misunderstanding, a sharp voice broke the uneasy quiet.

"Take your hands off her this instant, or so help me, I'll clip your ear hole so hard I'll knock you into next week!" Claire's Granny Greta stormed over, faithful Yorkshire Terrier, Spud, trotting by her side. Leslie instantly dropped her grasp, her jaw flapping like a bullying fish who'd just noticed the shark about to swallow her up. "Lay another finger on my Claire, and that threat won't stay one, you hear?"

Leslie grumbled in her throat as she returned to her stall, preoccupying herself with tweaking the angles of her cupcakes. Behind Greta, Alan shuffled to catch up with his walking cane.

"Trouble, little one?" he asked.

"This cheeky beggar just had hold of Claire!"

"It's nothing, Gran," Claire assured her, rubbing at her arm. "Just a little misunderstanding."

"I'll show her *misunderstanding*." Greta shook her fist above her head. What she lacked, thanks to her short Harris stature, she more than made up for in guts. "World's gone mad. Are you sure you're alright, Claire? I was going to take Spud for his morning walk around Starfall Park."

"I'm fine, honest." Claire kissed her on the cheek. "I'm lucky you were passing, but you get on with your walk."

"Hmm." Greta narrowed her eyes on Leslie again, still busy with her cupcakes. "Well, if I don't see you again, love, I'll see you tomorrow at the cul-de-sac for Christmas lunch. Your mother's not cooking the turkey again, is she?"

"I'm handling that, Mother," Alan said.

"Good." Greta nodded as she shuffled off. "Because last year, it was like eating reconstituted sawdust. Had to drown the poor bird in gravy after Janet murdered it for a second time, and don't even get me started on the potatoes…"

After reassuring her father she was fine and watching him head towards their candle stall, Claire retreated to her shop and the waiting wave of customers flooded in. Domino, one of Claire's cats, perched atop the counter, her eyes scanning the newcomers with feline curiosity. Sid had chosen to curl up in the flat upstairs, making Claire wish she could crawl under the covers to wake up on Christmas morning.

Claire's attention drifted back to the market as she attended to her first customer of the day, a woman whose basket overflowed with assorted candles. The woman moaned the pressure of office gift-giving, longing for simpler times when a Christmas card sufficed. Claire offered polite nods, but her gaze kept straying to the window.

She found Leslie Clark through the glass, still at her stall but casting occasional furtive glances towards the event tent. Leslie's earlier hostility lingered, nurturing a seed of suspicion that the fired chef was up to something. Then she noticed Grant Parker, the sous-chef from The Park Inn. Clad in plain clothes rather than his usual chef's whites, he loitered near the tent, an outsider to the day's events.

Another figure emerged from the tent as she handed the chattering customer her change. Marco ushered out an older man by the arm. Claire squinted, trying to place the familiar face. A flicker of recognition sparked at the sight of a head of lustrous, thick hair. Now silver, she could easily imagine it being the same auburn she'd seen atop Victor Michaels' head in the paper that morning.

The man with the thick hair wafted the tent away dismissively before slinking into the crowd. Like Grant the day before, Marco watched him leave with a shake of his head.

Claire's thoughts swirled with questions as she scanned and bagged on autopilot. The festive cheer of Northash was interwoven with an unmistakable tense undercurrent, and as the whispering hummed in the shop, Claire realised she was no longer alone in noticing it.

"Sooner that plum pudding publicity stunt is over and done with," a woman whispered to her as she snatched a receipt, "the better."

CHAPTER THREE

*L*ate afternoon light bathed the square as Claire Harris locked her candle shop to the background of the fading sun. Her boots crunched over frost-kissed cobbles as she passed the adjudicators waiting to be allowed into the tent, clipboards in gloved hands, faces a blend of sternness and curiosity. The afternoon following the strange morning had been quiet, and she wasn't sure she could take another outburst if they weighed in at nine-hundred-and-ninety-seven pounds.

She searched the crowd, landing on Ryan and the kids. They were huddled near the hot drinks van, each clasping a cup of hot chocolate.

"Ah, you made it," Ryan exclaimed as Claire

approached, his smile reaching his eyes. "Was beginning to think the shoppers wouldn't let you go."

"Almost cleared my shelves," she said, exhaling after the busy day. "But I wasn't going to miss this for anything."

Amelia hopped from foot to foot as she tried to peer at the tent over the crowd. Hugo, in typical Hugo fashion, was more interested in the digital world flashing on his handheld games console. Taking a hot chocolate from Ryan, Claire let the warmth spread through her fingers.

"How big is a tonne?" Amelia asked.

"Rhinoceroses," Hugo replied without looking up. "Car."

"*Cool*." Amelia's hopping turned to jumping. "Are they going to set it on fire like a proper Christmas pudding?"

Laughing, Claire scanned the packed market, landing on her satellite candle stall where her father, Alan, chatted with a customer. Granny Greta and Em were there too, their laughter echoing across the distance. Claire raised her hand, miming that she could go over and help. In response, Alan, illuminated by the soft flicker of candlelight, shook his head and flashed her a pinched forefinger and thumb 'okay' sign.

She returned to the event tent, where a hush began falling over the crowd. The moment they had all been waiting for was close at hand. The kids shuffled closer, and even Hugo had saved his game and tucked the console into his pocket.

"What if it *explodes*?" Amelia asked from atop Ryan's shoulders.

"Then a tonne of plum pudding will rain down on us," Claire replied, her stomach rumbling; alone in the shop, she'd skipped lunch. "Let's hope it doesn't. I'll settle for a job well done and a big fat slice on a plate."

"Oh, I think it's time," Ryan said, nudging Claire as the adjudicators stepped forward.

"Dad, I can't see," Hugo said, tugging his sleeve.

"I've only got one pair of shoulders, kiddo."

"Here." Claire crouched slightly, patting her back and leaving her hot chocolate on the floor. "I won't add much height to you, but it's worth a shot."

Hugo climbed aboard, and using Ryan to balance herself, Claire rose to her feet, clutching Hugo's gloved hands. As the adjudicators disappeared into the tent, the crowd's murmur swelled in anticipation, and then nothing. Five minutes passed, then ten, and the adjudicators still didn't emerge.

"A bald man is trying to get in!" Hugo announced. "He's being pushed back."

"A *bald* man?" Claire asked, tiptoeing but unable to see over the crowd that had doubled during the wait.

"That bloke is always shouting at the *other* pub,"

Amelia added. "And *that* man… he's always at the gym talking on his phone."

"What man?" Claire asked.

"Sounds like Tristan," Ryan answered for her. "He's never said two words to me, but he's in big business from what I've overheard from his conversations." He rubbed his fingers together as though to say 'money'. "Walks on the treadmill having business meetings through his headphones like he owns the place."

Letting Hugo down to the ground, Claire stepped out into the road to get a clearer view of the tent's entrance, where the two men were being barred entry by two chefs. The bald was Grant, and his gestures were sharp and animated, and beside him, Tristan, impeccably dressed in a black topcoat over a suit, stood with his arms folded, his face flushed with annoyance.

"This is a *joke!*" Grant's voice rose above the crowd, his tone laced with resentment. The sous-chef's words were sharp, slicing through the air with a tangible bitterness. "You'd be *nothing* without me!"

"Actually," Tristan declared, delivering to the crowd rather than the tent, "he'd be nothing without *me*. And I demand *immediate* repayment for funding this event!"

The surrounding crowd grew silent, the festive atmosphere dampened by the animosity. The revelation of financial strife added complexity to the already tangled web surrounding Chef Marco and his record attempt.

Grant, his face contorted with anger, seemed ready to retaliate, but the cooking helpers, their expressions stern, blocked his way with unwavering resolve. Tristan, meanwhile, stood seething, his demands echoing unanswered as Marco remained absent from the scene.

"When you overhear Tristan at the gym," Claire said to Ryan after she found him with the kids in the crowd. "You said he talks about money?"

"Seems to be some sort of investor," he said. "Spits out eye-watering figures like he's talking about the weather."

"So, not just a small-time local businessman?"

"He pays for the gym annually," Ryan added, as though that was all she needed to know. "An event like this must have cost a small fortune. Someone had to foot the bill."

Claire picked up her hot chocolate and sipped the sweet drink as she mulled over what she'd just witnessed. Tristan's claim that Marco would be 'nothing without' him carried some weight. But what about Grant's outburst? His words hinted at a personal stake, something beyond mere financial involvement.

For the second time that day, the sight of Leslie Clark, the fired chef, caught Claire's eye. She stood a short distance from the tent, checking her watch, her expression taut, eyes darting around as if waiting for someone… or something.

Claire then fell on another figure with a mane of grey hair, and after double-checking the picture on the

Observer website, she knew without doubt that the man was Victor Michaels. The current record holder leaned against the wall between her candle shop and the chippy next door. A hood concealed the top half of his face, but his thick hair couldn't be contained. Even without seeing his eyes, he was pointed at the tent.

"That's the guy who did it in 1987," Claire whispered to Ryan. "Saw him being marched out of the tent by Marco earlier. Doesn't seem too thrilled about Marco's attempt."

"Can't be easy watching someone challenge your claim to fame. What else has he done since?"

"Hadn't heard of him until these recent articles in the paper."

"Daaad," Amelia and Hugo whined together, as though rehearsed, their breath visible in the crisp evening air. "We're cold."

Claire looked down at the kids, their excitement now dampened by the chilly temperature. "Let's head over to The Hesketh Arms to warm up. There's no telling how long this will take."

Crossing the square, Claire passed her candle stall as it wound down for the day, and after making sure for a second time they didn't need help, she followed Ryan and the kids into the warmth of the pub. The kids cut to the pool table, Ryan following behind.

At the bar, Claire ordered drinks as the day's events

swirled. She wasn't sure why she cared so much. Maybe she'd been in the wrong place at the right time too often. If the record attempt had happened in Starfall House, where last year's market had taken place, or even on the other side of the clock tower, the titbits of drama might have passed her by.

"The whole thing's just a publicity stunt for The Park Inn," grumbled Malcolm Richards, one half of the couple who owned the bar, as he wiped down the surface with a well-used cloth. "Their fancy new chef with their fancy new menu… not very Northash, is it?"

Theresa Richards, his wife, nodded in agreement as she filled a second glass with a pint of Hesketh Homebrew. "It's like they're trying to put us out of business. Lucky the place is still as full as it is."

"True test will come in January when all the Christmas parties and pub crawls are over with," Malcolm said in a matter-of-fact tone. "We might be closed come spring if this keeps up. Can't compete."

"Can't compete," Theresa agreed.

"You don't need to," Claire said, leaning against the bar and offering a reassuring smile. "There's no replacing the charm of this place. Everyone knows *this* is the best pub, and there's no beating your home cooking."

"That's kind of you to say, Claire," Theresa replied, setting the pints on the mat before her. "On the house."

"Marco's the new flavour of the month," she assured

them. "You know what The Park Inn is like. They change their bar staff and menus as often as I change my window display. This place—" She patted the bar, toasting one of her free pints "—lasts."

"Well, let's hope you're right," Malcolm said, nodding his thanks as Claire tossed some coins into the tip jar. "Cross your fingers for us that Marco's stint in Northash is short-lived."

"Someone as fancy as that will get bored soon," Theresa agreed, staring off towards the 'other' pub. "Won't be around for much longer, I'm sure."

Malcolm slinked off, and Claire thanked Theresa for the free drinks and left the bar, balancing the tray of drinks as she made her way to their spot by the pool table. Amelia and Hugo were setting up for a game while Ryan chalked the cues. Claire slid the drinks tray onto the table and cracked her knuckles.

"Right then," she said, cracking her neck. "Who wants to lose first?"

Halfway through winning her first game against Ryan, a sudden scream from outside cut through the pub's festive hum. Sharp and panicked, it captured everyone's attention, and the scream didn't stop. Exchanging a quick, worried glance with Ryan, Claire moved swiftly towards the door.

"Guard the pool table," she ordered to the kids in a firm voice. "Pick up where we left off."

As she stepped outside, the cold air hit her, but the disordered scene unfolding in the square truly chilled her to the bone. Her mind raced with possibilities, each more worrying than the last, as she scanned the crowd for the source of the disturbance.

Outside, chaos had overtaken the square. Claire wove through the crowd, her heart racing.

"He's been *stabbed*!" she heard someone say.

"Stabbed in the *back*!"

"Is he *dead*?"

"How could someone survive *that*?"

As she neared the source of the commotion, Claire saw a woman with long, flowing hair dressed in bohemian clothing standing in shock near the back of the tent. In her trembling hands was a phone, but the wisps of her screaming were still making their way out. Her wide, horror-stricken eyes were fixed on something on the ground, her face as pale as the frost creeping up the clock tower.

Claire's eyes fell upon the harrowing sight following the woman's gaze. Chef Marco, the centre of the day's festivities, lay motionless, a knife jutting out of the centre of his back. His chef whites were white no longer as a red stain crept out, already pooled on the cobbles. His hand was curled around a lit cigarette, its smoke twisting lazily into the evening air.

As the breeze rustled the tent flaps, Claire caught a

glimpse of the giant plum pudding inside. The once anticipated glory was now overshadowed by the grim scene before her. The sweet aroma of the pudding, meant to symbolise celebration, now seemed grotesque.

"He's *dead*!" the woman wailed, searching the stunned faces of the crowd as they all watched on in disbelief. "Marco is *dead*."

Ryan touched Claire's arm, his voice low. "We should get the kids back to the flat. They don't need to see this."

Numb, Claire nodded. Ryan guided her back to the pub, and inside, she found Theresa behind the bar, face drained of colour, clutching the counter for support. From the back room burst

Malcolm, shirt untucked and wrinkled. He ran a hand over his hair and down his shirt, his breaths short and eyes wide. Theresa had been behind the bar when the scream had ruptured the air.

Where had Malcolm been?

CHAPTER FOUR

The Harris household, nestled in the heart of a sleepy cul-de-sac, twinkled like a constellation, a beacon of festive cheer on Christmas Day. Inside, Janet had transformed Claire's childhood home into an extravagant grotto, suffocated in tinsel, flashing lights, and three separate Christmas trees, each with a different colour scheme.

Seated at the dining table alongside Ryan, Amelia, Hugo, her parents, and Granny Greta, Claire watched as her father carved the crispy golden turkey.

The sight of the knife gliding through the succulent meat dragged forward an unwanted image to her mind—the knife jutting out of Marco's back. The knife in her memory had to be bigger than the real one... the pool of blood more prominent... the woman's scream louder...

Her stomach churned, unsure if she could eat the festive feast. She tried to focus on the laughter and chatter around the table and the warm glow of last year's candy cane candles flickering in the centre.

"You good?" Ryan whispered to her, his fingers wrapping around her thigh.

"Good," she replied, pushing forward a smile. "Looks delicious, Dad. Turkey looks perfect."

"Very juicy," Greta said, toasting her glass of sherry. "Did *you* make the potatoes, Janet?"

"I did, Greta."

"They look... very crispy." Greta squinted a smile as she toasted. "Get that meat on my plate, son. I could eat a goat!"

"You know what they say, Greta," Janet said as she loaded the shrivelled roast potatoes onto Greta's plate. "You are what you eat."

The traditional Christmas bickering relaxed Claire enough to sip buck's fizz.

"Now, everything is perfect," Janet said, scanning the table as she settled into her seat. "Everybody tuck in and —*napkins!*"

Claire trailed her mother into the kitchen, the air heavy with roasting meat and the lingering pine scent from the washing up her mother had already done from the cooking.

"Check that drawer," Janet ordered, flapping a finger

across the kitchen island. "We need the candy cane ones to match."

"Candy cane," Claire echoed. "Can I ask you something, Mum?"

"If you're going to get a dig in about my potatoes, I already know they're—"

"What do you make of what happened yesterday at the plum pudding attempt?"

"Oh." Janet paused, pulling out a stack of snowmen-themed napkins from the back of a drawer, her face softening before she stuffed them back. "It's concerning, dear. We're such a close-knit community. A tragedy like that is going to shake us all. I worry about the impact on everyone." Her eyes met Claire's, offering silent understanding. "But mostly you. You... *saw* Marco?"

Claire nodded as she continued rummaging. Her mother crossed the kitchen, her fingers closing around her arms in support. She picked the same spot Leslie had dug her nails in the day before.

"Try not to overthink it," she said, giving her one final squeeze. "Now, keep looking for those candy cane napkins. And I hope you've made a giant banner for your Boxing Day sale tomorrow. As the owner of a very *successful* cleaning business with ten staff, I know all about attracting customers, dear." She slammed another drawer before moving to the next one. "*Big... banner...*"

"Janet?" Alan called from the table. "Turkey's getting cold."

"And you won't have anything to wipe your fingers on if I don't find these napkins, dear," she called back. "Now, Claire, if you want a discount getting a banner, I clean the caravan of the guy who owns the print shop's cousin's friend, and he says…"

Claire half-listened, gazing at the frosty patterns on the window as her mother's voice blended with the background hum. Her mother's business advice—always unsolicited—seemed trivial amid the tragedy clouding her mind.

Janet continued, oblivious to Claire's distraction, confidently laying out a marketing strategy. "Visibility *is* key, Claire. You've got to make a splash, though it doesn't need to be perfect." She opened the first drawer again, grabbing the snowman napkins with a huff. "Right. *Christmas lunch!*"

Back at the table, Claire sank into her chair again between Ryan and Granny Greta while Greta topped up their glasses with more Baileys, eyes twinkling knowingly.

"You've got that look, Claire," she said. "The same one your father got when he was onto something in a case. Keep you awake last night?"

"I saw things, Gran," Claire confessed in a whisper. "Not just the knife. Things that could help solve

Marco's murder. But I don't know if I should get involved..."

"Trust yourself, dear. Your heart knows the way."

Alan sat at the head of the table, carving knife in hand, having just finished slicing the turkey. As he surveyed his family around the holiday spread, his expression grew distant, thoughts consumed by the Christmas Eve stabbing, no doubt.

Claire offered an encouraging smile, hoping to reassure him. Alan met her gaze and winked, raising his whisky glass, but the gaze returned as Janet took her seat after handing out the snowmen napkins. Claire wished they could discuss the case, but this wasn't the time or place.

"I *know* they don't match," Janet said as she pulled her seat in, tucking one into the collar of her candy cane Christmas jumper, "so, before you say anything, Greta—"

"You think I care about matching napkins?" Greta interrupted, tapping a blackened roast potato with her fork. "Pass the gravy, will you, Claire? I hope there's more than just that jug."

"Napkins, kids!" Janet ordered, pointing at her neck. "Don't want you ruining your new jumpers. A lot of time went into knitting those."

"You've taken up knitting?" Greta scoffed.

"Running a successful business, I don't have time to knit," Janet said, shaking out a napkin to cram over the edge of Hugo's collar. "But the nice lady I found on the online sales group did a splendid job, don't you think?"

"Lovely," Claire said, tugging at the one-size-too-small reindeer jumper she'd hopefully never have to wear again. "Funny how time repeats itself. Doesn't feel too long ago it was us, Ryan, having napkins crammed down our—"

Janet reached across Greta, cramming a napkin down Claire's collar, and knocked the gravy boat in Greta's hand. It sloshed onto the floor, licked up by Spud hiding under the table before Janet could clean it up.

"Shall we tuck in, dear?" Alan asked, already stabbing sprouts onto a fork. "Like my mother, I could also eat a goat or—"

"*Crackers!*" Janet cried.

As her mother rushed off, Claire couldn't hold her laughter back, and for the rest of the chaotic Christmas dinner, the events of Christmas Eve left her alone.

WITH FULL BELLIES AND HATS FROM THE CRACKERS crowning their heads, they migrated to the sitting room. Greta dozed in the armchair, paper crown tilted, while an old *The Great British Bake Off* Christmas special played on the television. Claire's mother buzzed about with a mini vacuum, sucking up stray crumbs. Amelia and Hugo lounged on the floor, engrossed in new gifts—a fancy colouring book and pens for Amelia and new 'skins' for his video game characters for Hugo.

Curled against Ryan on the sofa, Claire sunk into the contentment, the confusion of the last few days kept at bay. She looked around for her father but hadn't seen him since he'd slipped out fifteen minutes ago. Craning her neck, she glanced at the downstairs bathroom, but the door hung open.

The doorbell's chime echoed down the hallway, shattering the serenity of the sleepy early evening slump. Janet muttered under her breath about the audacity of an unannounced visitor as she hurried for the door. Awakened by the noise, Granny Greta's hand jerked, spilling her Baileys on the sofa arm.

"Oh, bother!" she whispered, dabbing the spill with her napkin, and when that only made matters worse, she dragged the blanket from her knee across the stain and closed her eyes again.

After some brief chatter at the front door, Detective Inspector Harry Ramsbottom lumbered in, decked in his winter coat, ho-ho-ho'ing in a cheerful but somewhat forced manner. Janet, her annoyance barely concealed behind a tight 'everything couldn't be more marvellous' smile, ushered him in.

"Merry Christmas, everyone!" he called around the room, gasping from the walk. "I didn't come empty-handed, I…" He reached into his pocket and pulled out a fistful of crushed candy canes. They went back in. "Oh, dear. I… I was hoping to have a word with Alan. In the kitchen, I presume?"

Without waiting for a response, Ramsbottom hobbled towards the kitchen, jingling the hallway tree.

"Christmas Day?" Janet muttered into the sitting room, her smile vanishing. "Who calls unannounced on *Christmas Day*?"

Claire, untangling herself from Ryan's embrace, made her way towards the kitchen, the festive sounds of the sitting room fading behind her.

In the kitchen, Janet surveyed her domain, apologising for the mess, though the table stood immaculate, wiped down and gleaming. The only remnants of their festive lunch were the plates of leftovers arranged neatly on the kitchen island, which caught DI Ramsbottom's eye as he scratched at his golden toupee.

"Fancy a plate, Harry?" Janet offered, her tone hovering between hospitality and challenge.

Ramsbottom's eyes twinkled at the invitation. "Oh, well, Mrs Ramsbottom put on a cracking Christmas lunch, but you know what Christmas Day is like." He chuckled, patting his belly, staining under his shirt. "Might as well have as many stomachs as a cow."

"*Just* Christmas Day?" Janet muttered under her breath as she handed him a plate. "Please, help yourself."

He began piling it high with turkey, roast potatoes, and the trimmings. Janet watched, her lips pressing into a thin line as her 'throw it all in a Boxing Day soup' leftovers vanished.

The detective, oblivious to Janet's pursed lip glare, savoured the sight of the piled-high plate as he drowned it in the rest of the gravy.

Claire, her curiosity piqued, leaned towards Ramsbottom as he dived in with a knife and fork at the island. "Any updates on the investigation?"

Ramsbottom, chewing, nodded and said, "Marco was indeed stabbed. No prints on the knife, which suggests premeditation." He paused to cram in more turkey. "He was out the back between the tent and the clock tower having a cheeky cigarette break while those record people with clipboards weighed the pudding." He paused, his gaze distant momentarily, before eating a stuffing ball whole. "You know what's funny? All that effort, and he was *still* five pounds away from Victor's record." He laughed. "Still, I suppose it's a small mercy he didn't live to see his failure, right?"

"Small mercies," Janet said flatly as she gathered the leftover leftovers onto a single plate.

"So, it had to be someone already in the tent?" Claire

asked, mulling over the information as thoroughly as Ramsbottom was chewing a pig in a blanket.

"Not necessarily. Between the tent and the clock tower was a private area for Hugo to slip off for a smoke when things got too stressful. Private, but not impenetrable. Only made of vinyl, anyone could have lifted it up to sink that blade between his…" He mimicked the motion with his knife before stabbing up more turkey. "Terrible, terrible business."

"Anyone," Claire repeated with a nod. "Anyone who knew he'd be out there smoking, and someone who had to know there was an 'out there' there in the first place."

"Great point!" Ramsbottom jabbed the fork in her direction. "And we've been looking into your claim about the missing knife. Can't confirm anything yet, but the knife that killed him was a paring knife like you said."

"Like Marco said," she remembered aloud. "And according to him, he didn't lose it, which means someone took it."

As he topped up his food with the last drops of gravy, Janet, ever the hostess—even when unwilling—placed a cracker and a candy cane napkin beside him; she'd found them at the back of the drink's cabinet after they'd finished eating. Ramsbottom, with a slight chuckle, offered the cracker to Claire. It cracked in her favour, but she handed him the yellow paper hat. He placed it atop his toupee, a splash of festive colour against the gold.

"Go on, read us the joke, Claire."

Claire unfolded the small slip of paper and read aloud, "Why was the snowman looking through the carrots?" She paused, a smile playing on her lips. "He was picking his nose."

Ramsbottom slapped the counter, his bellowing laugh turning into a cough that lasted long enough for Claire to pat him on the back. Janet placed a glass of water beside him, tidying up the cracker debris on her way.

"About the knife," Claire continued as he gulped down the water. "There's more I didn't mention when I called the station earlier. I saw someone hanging around those knives two days ago."

Ramsbottom leaned forward into the spotlights above the island, his face glowing yellow as the light shone through the paper crown. Behind him and through the window, Claire noticed a similar hue glowing from the shed at the bottom of the garden. Claire recounted the scenes she had witnessed, each detail vivid. She spoke of the sous-chef's heated departure from the tent. Her voice lowered as she recalled Leslie's frustrated conversation, her words laced with bitterness towards Marco.

"And don't forget the assault!" Janet called over her shoulder as the foil-wrapped leftovers went into the fridge. "You could have her arrested. Or *sue* her. That'll pay for your sale banner."

"She grabbed me. She accused me of eavesdropping."

Claire paused, collecting her thoughts before continuing. "I *was* eavesdropping, just not that time. But I'll let it slide. There was Victor, too."

"The previous record holder?" Ramsbottom nodded. "Or should I say, current record holder? He'll be happy. Heard he wasn't too pleased that his title might be snatched."

"That's just it," Claire said, leaning closer. "I saw *him* too. He was being escorted out of the tent by Marco. It was less tense than I witnessed with Grant, but neither looked happy. And then I saw him again staring at the tent not long before Marco was stabbed. Leslie too. And Grant was there shouting the odds. And then there's Tristan..." She hesitated, recalling the businessman's demanding tone. "He was insistent about being repaid, almost as if Marco was avoiding him. I think he might have been the investor behind the event. I have it on good authority that he's a rich investor."

"Questioned everyone in the vicinity," Ramsbottom remarked around a mouthful. "Including those pub owners across the way. Wanted their whereabouts accounted for." He tapped his temple knowingly. "The husband claims he didn't leave the pub, but eyewitnesses say Theresa was alone behind the bar around that time. I don't want to speak out of turn, but I heard they weren't taking the competition well..." He shook his head as though he didn't want to believe it. "But your observations of Tristan are very insightful, Claire. These interactions could be significant. So far, our focus has been on Elena."

"Elena?" Claire echoed.

"The hippie lass who found him," Ramsbottom confirmed, and the echo of her scream resounded in Claire's memory as she connected the name to the woman who'd been standing over his body. "His girlfriend. Explains why she knew where to find him. He'd only been dead a couple of minutes at that point. If only she'd got there sooner."

"Who says she didn't?" Janet called out, waving a knife as she transferred it from the straining board to slide it into the knife block. "If my Alan doesn't come out of that shed soon…"

"Speaking of which, I would still like to talk to him," he said, pushing the plate away. "That was wonderful, Janet. Sorry I couldn't finish it, but I couldn't possibly eat another thing."

"Not to worry." Picking up the plate, Janet glared at the two roast potatoes he'd left behind before dumping them in the bin.

"Here, Claire?" he said as he shuffled to the back door. "Would you mind keeping your eyes peeled? You've got that same insightful knack your father had back when he had my job."

Claire watched him walk down the garden path to the

shed, her mind a whirlwind of conflicting emotions. She leaned against the island as her mother polished the marble with glass cleaner, a deep sigh escaping her lips—and she saw it in the marble once it had been polished to a mirror finish.

"What do I do, Mum?" Claire asked as a fresh glass of buck's fizz appeared before her. "You're good at sorting up messes."

"I know *exactly* what you should do," Janet said, clicking her fingers together. "Call that banner place first thing in the morning. I think I have a business card somewhere…"

Feeling no more transparent—and sure she couldn't get a banner printed at such short notice—Claire sipped the buck's fizz and hoped the answer awaited her at the bottom of the glass.

IN THE QUIET OF THE EVENING, WITH AMELIA AND HUGO settling in the guest room, Ryan in the shower, and Granny Greta on her way home with Janet behind the wheel, Claire felt the irresistible pull towards her father's garden shed. The shed, a quaint wooden hut in the corner of the garden, had been the backdrop of many significant moments in her life. Its familiar scent of potting soil and petrol from the lawnmower soothed her unsettled thoughts.

She found her father inside, his hands busy taking clippings of a vibrant red poinsettia plant. He looked up, his face breaking into a smile at the sight of Claire.

"Thought I might find you in here."

"Evening, little one," he said, accepting a mug of Horlicks. "Splash of Baileys?"

"What do you take me for? It's Christmas, isn't it?"

He laughed, taking the first sip as Claire settled onto the upturned terracotta plant pot in the corner. She must have sat on the same pot at least once a week since she was knee high.

"Been thinking about it?" she asked.

"Mmhmm." He took a long sip before setting down the mug and wiping his hands on a rag. "Seems a lot is going on beneath the surface of this case. I might have something that could help you decide. Your mother and I were trying out the *new* Park Inn last week, and we inadvertently overheard something Harry thinks might be a big clue. The tail-end of that argument you overheard between Marco and Grant wasn't the first."

Leaning closer, Claire said, "Oh?"

"Grant stormed out of the kitchen and threw his chef's hat off as you witnessed." He twisted in the dirty office chair and hooked his arm over the back. "In front of the packed pub, Grant claimed he was behind the entire menu at The Park Inn. He said all the new

49

recipes were *his* idea. Said the plum pudding stunt was *his* idea."

"Grant in the brainchild behind Marco?"

"Or so he claims," he confirmed. "And Marco didn't argue the fact. He laughed awkwardly as he snatched Grant's hat after the sous-chef left. He told us all to enjoy our food and bowed out. They must have made up again if Grant was in the tent the day before Christmas Eve like you saw."

"But whatever friction lay between them wasn't resolved." Claire's eyes widened. The implications of her father's revelations added another layer. The possibility that Marco's pursuit of fame had overshadowed Grant's creative efforts stirred a sense of injustice in her. "Prime suspect?"

He assessed her with a curious smile. "Are you thinking of investigating, little one?"

Claire hesitated like she had when asked by Ramsbottom earlier in the evening. Her instincts urged her to dive into the investigation, to unravel the mystery that had cast a shadow over Northash. Yet, the responsibility of her business, her commitment to the candle shop, and the upcoming sale anchored her in reality.

"I'll be busy with the shop," she finally said, her voice unwavering. "The Boxing Day sale..."

Alan nodded with an understanding smile, but his

brows drifted up as the smile grew more playful. "That wasn't a *no*, little one."

BACK IN THE SITTING ROOM, WITH JANET STILL NOT BACK from driving Granny Greta home and the kids fast asleep, Claire nestled into Ryan's side, damp from the shower and smelling like peppermint.

"As lovely as today was, I'm glad we can tick Christmas off the list," he said, his voice a balm against her ear before he kissed her forehead. "You should take those Christmas cards of mine off your shop walls. Season's over."

Claire pulled back from the hug, catching his crooked smile that awakened the butterflies anew, even now.

"Oh no, you won't wiggle out of our deal that easily," she said. "I'm keeping them up through New Year, I told you. I bet every last one sells by the first day of January."

"Is that a wager I hear?" At Claire's defiant chin lift, he laughed. "Fine, if all the cards sell, I'll bet you a tenner, but you're already down twenty for the plum pudding not beating the record."

Claire tilted her head, smile slowly spreading. "Alright, if all the cards sell, I don't want your money... I want you to submit a piece of work to that little gallery a few doors down from Marley's." Ryan opened his mouth to protest, but she pressed on. "The same way I had to believe in my candles, you need to have some faith in that talent of yours, Ryan. I love you too much not to push you to try."

Ryan ran a hand through his hair, hints of silver glinting at his sandy temples. "Claire, I'm a hobbyist. Not like real gallery types."

But Claire held out her hand expectantly, determination etched on her face. "A deal's a deal, Ryan Tyler. I've known you too long to know you'll never advocate for yourself regarding your art. You were shy about it when we were kids, too, and you were head and shoulders above anyone our age."

Ryan clasped her outstretched hand with a resigned chuckle, lighting up a spark of joy like New Year's fireworks.

"Well, businesswoman, since you have me at your mercy, what now?" Ryan said. "We attack that leftover box of chocolates until we feel sick? Or maybe..." He leaned in, warm breath caressing her ear once more. "...we turn in early tonight?"

She traced a finger along his stubbled jaw. "Best save our energy. The gym will be just as busy as my shop with madcaps wanting to burn off the Christmas calories."

Laugh lines creased Ryan's eyes as he drew her close. "My clever Claire. You do have the best ideas." His lips found hers, firm and seeking, as he led her towards the stairs. The kiss deepened until Claire was breathless.

As she ascended the familiar creaking steps towards her childhood bedroom, Claire knew Ryan was right in one respect. The Christmas chaos was ending at last. But as for what tomorrow and the week before the new year might bring—her business, her home, her beloved village —those mysteries still awaited unravelling. For now, she let her doubts fade into Ryan's searing kiss, allowing herself to be. If only for this moment.

Tomorrow, she'd need a pair of fighting mitts to tackle Boxing Day.

CHAPTER FIVE

oxing Day ushered in a flurry of activity within Claire's Candles. The shop, still decked out for Christmas, buzzed with a swarm of customers drawn in by the promise of discounts. Buy One Get One Free on all festive candles *and* another twenty percent off across all ranges. She knocked a pound off the Christmas cards, too, determined to win her bet with Ryan after losing the plum pudding one so spectacularly.

With Damon by her side, Claire attended to each customer with a smile, keeping the mystery of Marco's murder at bay as much as she could. She guided them through her candles' scents and burn times, each recommendation tailored to their needs. Her expertise shone as she paired fragrant jasmine with cosy reading nooks and rich cinnamon with bustling kitchens. The till chimed in a steady rhythm, marking sales as fast as Damon could keep the shelves stocked.

But the murder was never too far from popping up, and Claire's gaze often strayed to the window. The giant white kitchen tent, a remnant of Christmas Eve's unfortunate event, stood as a black spot on a successful day in the shop.

"Still can't believe it, can you?" Damon asked, his voice barely above a whisper as he restocked the bags behind the counter. "Who murders someone on Christmas Eve?"

"A sous-chef," Claire thought aloud. "Or an investor. A replaced chef, or how about a record holder? And then there's the girlfriend… And the rival pub owners…"

"So, that answers my *next* question. You've been thinking about it, then?"

"A little."

"A *little*?" Damon laughed, reaching around her to refill the till with more rolls. "You have a whole list of suspects."

The bell above the door jingled, announcing new customers, pulling Claire back to the present. She turned, her professional mask in place, ready to welcome another batch of shoppers. Yet, her thoughts remained tethered to the tent outside, a silent sentinel of the mystery that had disrupted their peaceful village life.

Eugene Cropper, Marley's husband, known for his

dramatic flair and not one to shy away from scandal, led the charge of the second wave, leaning conspiratorially over the counter, his baritone whisper a blend of intrigue and disbelief.

"I heard Marco's girlfriend, Elena, found him," Eugene whispered, his eyes wide with drama. "Covered in blood, she was. Right in the middle of the kitchen tent. Can you imagine?"

Claire, her hands busily wrapping a set of frosted plum candles, raised an eyebrow at the incorrect details, but she didn't correct him. If she did, she'd become the subject of an interrogation; somehow, the news she'd seen the body hadn't spread, and she was one of only a handful from the sounds of things.

"And that woman he replaced at the other pub?" he continued, his voice gruff with suspicion. "Was shouting down the phone about ruining his record attempt, and no one knows who she was talking to, and I heard Elena ended things with Marco."

Claire's head whipped around. "When?"

"The night before his death," he said. "Why was *she* the first on the scene to find him?"

"It's that sous-chef, Grant," someone else chimed in, a regular Claire recognised but whose name escaped her. "Always seemed jealous of Marco. Maybe he couldn't take it anymore."

Another customer, lingering near the star candle

display, added, "And don't forget Leslie. She never hid her disdain for Marco after he took her place at The Park Inn."

"I overheard Malcolm and Theresa going at it something fierce in the pub kitchen last night," Eugene said. "They're still furious over Marco stealing all their business, even with him dead. Claim the stunt was an underhanded tactic. It's taken years to build Hesketh's reputation. They wouldn't let Marco destroy it without a fight."

"You don't think..." someone gasped.

"I'm not saying they *would*," Eugene's voice dropped to a whisper, "but I *did* hear that Malcolm's whereabouts at the time of the murder are still unverified..."

As the conversation continued, Claire was drawn into the river of rumour. The theories, each more elaborate than the last, painted a picture of a village rife with hidden tensions and unresolved conflicts.

And yet, only one new detail.

Elena dumped Marco the night before his death.

"Damon?" she began when they were in the stockroom together as the coffee machine ground up a fresh batch of beans for midday espressos. "What do I do?"

Damon paused, setting aside a candle he'd been labelling. His expression mirrored Claire's concern.

"If this were a game, I'd say it was set to extra difficult

mode," he said. "Or if you were The Doctor, this would be a Dalek episode. It's a tricky one, alright."

"And if I was Claire from the candle shop?" she asked, pleading with her eyes for him to be straightforward. "You said it yourself... I have all these suspects... and I *suspect* them."

"Funny that."

She whacked his arm as the machine dripped the aromatic coffee into the tiny cups. "Be a mate and tell me what to do, yeah?"

"Is that what mates do?"

"Be an *employee* and tell me what to do."

He smiled. "Or you'll fire me?"

"Exactly."

Damon accepted the first cup of espresso, cradling it in his hands as he craned his neck to check on the shop. Seemingly satisfied that they weren't being robbed blind, he leaned in.

"I *did* hear something at the café," he started in a low, strained voice. "I was returning to my flat after a convention, and Victor was there. I didn't know him from Adam then, but after you mentioned his..." He motioned to a big bush of hair. "...how many men in their sixties have that much left? Sally said I'm thinning on top. What do you think?"

He bowed his head and sighed. Claire gave it a little

rummage, and then she brushed the hairs back over the sight of his scalp.

"Looks fine to me," she assured him. "What did you overhear that made it stick in your mind if you didn't know who he was?"

"Old bloke was grumbling about Marco, saying something about him trying to 'steal his glory', which has to be the plum pudding record attempt, right?" He sipped the hot coffee, wincing as it burned his tongue. "Eugene mentioned he used to own a restaurant somewhere around here."

"Did I hear my name?" Eugene called, letting himself behind the counter and into the storeroom. He gave it a once over before leaning in to join them. "Little place called Victor's. Where that new little gallery is, it was quite a classy place. That gigantic plum pudding brought him a lot of attention, but gimmicks don't last forever, do they? Was closed by the new millennium, and I haven't heard a peep from Victor until those articles about someone wanting to break his record started popping up a few months ago."

Claire leaned against the counter as she absorbed the new information. Victor's fall from culinary acclaim to obscurity and his apparent bitterness towards Marco painted a portrait of a man clinging to past glories. It explained his lingering presence over the last few days.

"This feels crucial," Claire said, her detective instincts

fully awakened. "Victor's motive couldn't be clearer. His pride and legacy were at stake."

Damon tossed back the rest of his espresso and said, "Since you saved me from hitting the slopes with Sally, I owe you one. She couldn't think of what to get her mum, so she's taken her with the girls instead. I'm all yours to handle the shop."

Still deep in thought about Victor's potential motives, Claire barely registered Damon's offer.

"*Claire?*" Eugene clicked before her eyes, pushing her cup from the machine into her hands. "That means down this to get those cogs working, and then get your beautiful behind to that white tent before the place shuts down. Ramsbottom was scratching his toupee bare when he entered the café for breakfast. He won't turn you away."

Claire remained rooted in the storeroom for a moment before she tossed the coffee back like a mechanical response. It burned on the way down, clearing any tiredness still lingering from dragging herself out of her childhood bed that morning.

"Ten minutes," she conceded. "A bit of fresh air and a poke around the tent might do me some good."

Claire donned her coat and stepped out into the brisk Boxing Day air. Making her way towards the tent, she had no idea what she was about to walk into.

CHAPTER SIX

*C*laire slipped into the tent as the winter breeze opened the entrance in an inviting flutter. Inside, the unfinished plum pudding loomed as large as a rhino—or small car—a memorial to ambition now steeped in disaster. As delicious as it smelt, it looked like it had started to congeal.

DI Ramsbottom sauntered amidst the chaos, scanning the scene with methodical precision as his uniformed officers poked around. His gaze lifted to meet Claire's, a smile lifting his stern expression.

"Ah, Claire! Your father with you?" he greeted, looking around her. "No matter. Your knack for finding yourself in the heart of Northash's mysteries precedes you once again. Thought you'd hung up your hat after that springtime mess at the garden centre earlier this year."

"Me too," she replied, her eyes briefly meeting Ramsbottom's before shifting back to the pudding. The sight of it, as tremendous as it was and still a few pounds underweight, symbolised the abrupt end to Marco's aspirations and life: the fine line between success and downfall, joy and despair, delicious and deadly.

In the shadow of the colossal pudding, Elena sat on the other side of the tent, her knees drawn to her chest, hugging herself on the counter into a small ball. She had the same confused stare she'd had looking over Marco's body, marred by grief, eyes red-rimmed and distant as she stared through her boyfriend's—or ex-boyfriend's—pudding.

"Been here all morning," Ramsbottom whispered. "I tried to move her on, but the poor lass was distraught. Didn't want to arrest her, so..."

Ramsbottom nodded for Claire to have a go, so she walked around the pudding, her steps quiet on the canvas floor. Elena trembled slightly in her clutched hunch, stare not leaving the pudding. She looked shattered in more ways than one.

Claire edged closer to Elena, her decision firming with each step. The metal frame creaked under their combined weight as she hoisted herself beside Elena on the counter. She flashed a wry smile.

"Not my brightest idea. I could probably do with getting down."

Elena's hand shot out, her bangles jangling in a chorus of metallic whispers, gripping Claire's wrist. "Stay, please."

Claire's gaze lingered on their clasped hands, feeling the weight of Elena's touch. Settling on the metal, she waited for it to collapse beneath them. A relieved breath escaped her when it didn't budge.

"I saw you yesterday," Elena murmured, her eyes meeting Claire's with fragile intensity. "You were one of the few not just *staring* at... Marco."

Claire's nod was subtle, returning the hand squeeze with a silent promise of solidarity. She kept to herself that she'd done her fair share of staring—enough that the bloody chef's whites had yet to leave her mind.

"You're Marco's girlfriend?" Claire ventured.

Elena's eyes flickered, a shadow of pain crossing her features, and she corrected, "*Ex*-girlfriend."

"Ah."

A sigh escaped Elena's lips as if unburdening a weight, and as Elena mulled over her thoughts, Claire remained silent, offering space for Elena's story to unfold. She sensed a gateway opening to an honest conversation. Many would have kept such a detailed secret given how close to his murder she'd ended things; at least the gossip wasn't all talking hot air back at the shop.

"I left Marco because of this *stupid* thing." She nodded at the pudding with a snarl on her upper lip. "Marco was convinced it would all be worth it in the end. Fame, fortune, glory... but he was blind to what he already had. A good job, friends... *me*." She sniffed back tears. "He was willing to risk it all to break an old record. Nobody even remembered it until he made his big announcement in the pub."

"A tale as old as time," Ramsbottom announced. "Ambition clouding judgment, overshadowing the things that gave life meaning."

Elena's hands tightened around Claire's, the bangles clinking softly, echoing in the vast tent.

"He was *consumed* by the record," Elena continued, her voice barely above a whisper. "It was all he could talk about, all he cared about. Our relationship... it just couldn't compete with his obsession." A single tear trailed down her cheek, glistening like a diamond in the dim light. "I wasn't enough for him. I wasn't... I wasn't a giant plum pudding!"

Elena caught Claire's eye, and she couldn't hold back her laugh at the absurdity despite Claire biting back her lips. Elena sighed and let out a strained laugh.

"You're right," Elena said. "It's ridiculous. But I thought I loved him, and now he's..." She looked off to the back of the tent where the forensic officers were concentrated. "Stabbed in the back. Who'd do something like that?"

Claire looked off to Ramsbottom on the other side of

the pudding, and he'd been watching them for their whole conversation. She remembered what he'd said when they were in her parents' kitchen on Christmas Day; he'd thought Elena was the lead suspect, but Claire wasn't so sure.

"That's what we need to figure out," Claire said, nudging Elena's shoulder with hers. "You must have known Marco better than most. Who do *you* think killed him?"

Before Elena could respond, the flap of the tent rustled, and Grant, the sous-chef, entered. His arrival cast a sudden chill over the space, and Elena's reaction was immediate; her body tensed, and she averted her gaze from Grant.

"I… I need to go," she murmured, almost to herself.

With her head bowed, she slid away from Claire and brushed past Grant, who reached out, attempting to engage her.

"Elena, *wait*! Let's talk."

Grant's words were brushed aside as Elena, shaking with silent sobs, breezed past him and out into the cold. Claire exchanged a glance with Ramsbottom and raised her eyebrows in a silent question, but Ramsbottom nodded, encouraging her to approach Grant. Despite her hesitation, recalling Grant's earlier outburst when he caught her peeping into the tent, Claire knew she had a chance to talk to her personal prime suspect.

"Might as well," she whispered, hopping off the counter.

Walking towards Grant, she prepared to navigate the fragile terrain of his temper and the mystery beneath, but Grant was focused on something else. He leaned over and grabbed a bag stashed under the counter.

"Excuse me!" Ramsbottom called. "You can't touch that."

"I've just come to collect my stuff," he said. "Just my gym clothes."

"I'm afraid it could be evidence until we say otherwise."

"My stinky socks are evidence?" Grant scoffed, folding his thick arms. Ramsbottom nodded an apology, and the sous-chef huffed. "Fine. Whatever. Keep it. See if I care."

Grant turned on his heel to leave, but Claire, driven by curiosity, followed him out of the tent. He paused, turning to look at her with a mix of surprise and suspicion.

"You," he said. "You were spying."

"Just passing," she said. "And maybe snooping a little. I was just curious about the pudding. I... I'm sorry for your loss."

"Did you know Marco?'" he said, a bite to his voice.

Claire shook her head. "Not really."

"Then you wouldn't be sorry if you'd known him. *Truly* known him."

"And did you know Marco, Grant?"

His eyes narrowed. "Why are you asking me all these questions? What, you think I have something to hide?"

The defensiveness in his voice struck Claire, confirming her suspicions that there was more to Grant's story. Why say that unless there was something to hide? Seizing the conversation shift, Claire decided she'd need to pivot to safer territory before he performed another dramatic exit.

"You worked with him at the pub," she stated, nodding around the corner. "I heard there was some tension between you and Marco. It must've been challenging working under such conditions."

Grant's expression tightened, a clear sign Claire had struck a nerve with her vague comment. He hesitated, then sighed, his shoulders sagging.

"Yeah, it was challenging, alright," he admitted, though he stopped short of openly confessing his frustrations. "Marco was a pain to work for. He always smiled at customers, but was a different man in the kitchen. Tough, arrogant... downright rude."

Claire could have said the same about Grant, but she *had* witnessed Marco barking at his staff over the missing knife.

"I heard about the scene at the restaurant," Claire said.

"What scene?"

"When you quit last week."

He shrugged. "Dunno what you're talking about."

"It's public knowledge, Grant. You voiced your concerns quite openly in front of a packed restaurant. Accused Marco of stealing your ideas for the menu? For his record attempt?" She ducked to meet his avoiding gaze, but he only looked further down. "Any truth to that?"

He glanced away towards the park, jaw clenching. "Marco always took more than his share of things."

Claire noted Grant's reluctance to admit he was the brainchild behind Marco, but she trusted her father's version of the story. He'd given her something, though. More than his fair share? Claire filed away the insight. For now, Grant still hadn't marched off.

"Why did you storm out and not participate in the record attempt? It must have been important to you?"

"Creative differences," he spat out, the words laced with contempt. "Marco wouldn't listen when I told him the record attempt would fail. And according to the police, it was under, like I said. But Marco wouldn't listen. He never listened unless you said something he could claim he thought of first. It was always about *him*. *His* fame, *his* record." His hands clenched into fists by his side. "Whatever. He got what he deserved, didn't it?"

"Stabbed, you mean?" Claire pushed. "With a missing paring knife, wasn't it?"

"What of it?"

"I saw you," she admitted, taking a step closer. "By the knife blocks. You looked like you were up to something."

Grant laughed to himself, shaking his head. Without another word, he turned abruptly and walked off towards the park. As he left, Claire was sure she heard him muttering about "nosey busybodies" under his breath.

As she watched him round the corner at the post office, Claire couldn't help but feel that Elena, with her raw grief and vulnerability, seemed far removed from the crime. On the other hand, with his barely contained resentment and evasive answers, Grant appeared far from innocent.

And the timing of Elena's exit—leaving at the sight of the sous-chef—couldn't have been a coincidence. There was something between them that needed exploring.

Back in the tent, Claire re-joined DI Ramsbottom in the shadow of the pudding. He hunched over a table with Marco's belongings, his eyes scrutinising a cluster of financial documents. Claire peered over his shoulder while Ramsbottom's fingers traced the numbers. The sheet he studied was a loan agreement from a certain Tristan Raybourn.

"Would that be the same Tristan demanding to see Marco before his death?" Claire asked.

"The very same, and it seems your hunch was correct. Marco owed quite the sum to this Tristan fellow," he said. "Twenty thousand, to be exact. Money for purchasing equipment, ingredients, publicity... all for the record attempt."

"Twenty thousand?" Claire whistled, glancing at the cursed pudding. "Seems a bit steep for a publicity stunt. Explains why Tristan claimed Marco would be 'nothing' without him."

Ramsbottom nodded, his gaze still fixed on the papers. "Indeed. Tristan's financial hold over Marco adds another layer to this puzzle. Something we—I mean I— need to look into. Did you get much from those two?"

"Elena confirmed she ended things with Marco, but I don't think she's your suspect," she said, looking off to the counter where they'd been sitting. "Grant, on the other hand... he's being evasive, and you saw how Elena reacted when he showed up. I think there might be something there. Have you looked through his bag?"

"Gym stuff, like he said," Ramsbottom said with a huff, still reviewing the records. "And he's right. Those socks do... *Hello*, what's this?"

Ramsbottom tugged out a crinkled page that immediately seemed out of place in the mix of spreadsheets and documents—a hand-drawn sketch of a plum pudding. Detailed with scribbled dimensions and a recipe, the drawing resembled the plum pudding watching over them. The handwriting was elegant and slightly faded, reminding Claire of Granny Greta's writing.

Intrigued, Claire leaned closer, her eyes narrowing as she examined the measurements. The recipe called for shocking quantities like 5000 kg of breadcrumbs, flour, suet, brown sugar, mixed dried fruits, and 2500 kg of chopped candied peel and chopped spiced Damson plums. Other measurements were equally extreme, including 100 kg of mixed spice and 25 kg of ground ginger.

"This must be Marco's sketch for the giant pudding," Ramsbottom murmured, pointing to a line that read: 'inspired by '87' in the corner. "But why make something so close to the record-breaking one from 1987 when it failed to reach the tonne?" He ran his fingers over the paper, grumbling in his throat before tilting it to the light. "Curious."

"What is it?" she asked.

"It seems there are indents from more writing, like something was written overtop this page..."

While Ramsbottom scribbled in his pad, officers carefully placed the sketch and other paperwork into evidence bags, meticulously preserving each item. Claire stepped out of the tent, the winter air biting her cheeks.

The discovery of the sketch amongst Marco's

belongings had ignited a determination within her to unravel the mystery that had enveloped Northash.

The stakes were as high as the giant pudding, not just for justice for Marco but for the community entwined in the tragedy.

Laughter ceased when eyes drifted to the tent.

Smiles flipped to solemn frowns.

Gossip lowered several decibels.

Marco's murder was a spectre in the shadow of the most wonderful time of year, and something had to be done to set things right before New Year.

Rather than head straight back to the shop, Claire pivoted to the gym across the square. She found Ryan restacking the weights in the gym, which was as busy as she'd predicted, with most of the machines filled with people pushing themselves to their limits, faces as red and sweaty as Santa himself.

"I'm on the case, Ryan," she said after a quick kiss. "There's too much weird stuff going on to ignore."

Ryan, wiping sweat from his brow, flashed her a supportive smile. "Then I suppose I'll have to be your little sidekick," he joked, but his eyes held a seriousness that mirrored Claire's own. "And I think I can help with one of your suspects. Tristan usually comes in around now. Maybe the murder and Christmas have disrupted his routine, but..."

His words trailed off as he nodded towards the door.

Claire turned to see Tristan stride in all suited up, a gym bag slung over his shoulder, his usual air of authority undiminished by recent events. The timing was uncanny, presenting an opportunity Claire knew she couldn't pass up.

"Treadmills, right?" she asked as Tristan headed to the changing rooms. "Mind if I jump on next to him?"

"I do," he replied, clenching an eye. "Only clients are insured, and as the manager of this fine establishment *and* your boyfriend, I can't let you get on in case you slip."

"I won't…" She glanced at the treadmills as a row of limber stick insects sprinted towards an invisible goal. "Okay, good point. I'll have to become a client, won't I?"

"You want to… *join*?"

"Don't look so shocked," she said, whacking his washboard abs. "And whatever you do, don't tell my mother. She'll only get excited." Hands on her hips, she copied a woman by the lockers by pivoting her hips from side to side. "What was that offer Em told me about? Same Year, New Me?"

CHAPTER SEVEN

*C*laire waited impatiently in the changing room, tapping her foot as she stared at the door Tristan had just exited through. She was eager to put her hastily constructed plan into action. Though joining the gym had been a spur-of-the-moment—and out-of-character—idea, she knew this was her chance to get Tristan alone and gather intel.

After an eternity, Claire emerged in an oversized t-shirt and leggings, feeling utterly exposed. She cringed as she caught her reflection in the mirror—the shapeless clothes did little to flatter her figure. With a sigh, she reminded herself that solving Marco's murder took priority over her insecurities.

She stepped onto the gym floor, scanning the sea of treadmills for Tristan. She spotted his towering frame pounding away on a machine near the back, eyes fixed on a mounted TV screen. His authoritative presence dominated the surrounding space, even with wireless headphones clamped in his ears. Claire noted his muscular physique in his tight workout clothes could overpower a man like Marco.

Unsure how to approach, Claire claimed the only free elliptical machine nearby. As she wobbled her feet back and forth, she fixed her eyes on Tristan, trying to discern any information she could gather at a distance. Besides his rapid footwork and focused stare ahead, Tristan offered little in revealing body language until he began speaking. His voice carried over the drone of the gym as though he were in his office. Craning her neck, Claire realised he must be on a hand-free call. She slowed her elliptical pace, straining to make out his conversation.

"Yes, I want the order from the brewery in the first quarter of next year," Tristan bellowed. "And those pub makeovers we discussed? Bring it forward. Summer is too far. Strip *everything* out. Get rid of the old and bring in the new. This is a game of survival by *any* means."

Claire's ears perked up. She wondered if one of those pubs included The Park Inn, confirming Tristan's investment. As Tristan ended his call, the treadmill beside him opened up. Heart pounding nearly as fast as her feet, Claire seized the opportunity.

Crossing the gym floor, she mounted the treadmill,

gripping the handrails for support. The machine hummed to life at the push of a button, propelling her feet backwards. Panicked, Claire grappled for the controls, casting her mind back to the few times she'd been forced onto a treadmill during her weekly gym excursions in high school; if only she hadn't spent so much time bouncing up and down on the yoga balls with Sally.

"Excuse me?" she whispered to Tristan as he sprinted ahead. "I'm not quite sure how to work this. Could you help me figure it out? I'm new here."

Tristan slowed his run down with a few jabs of the console, his eyes lingering on Claire's soft curves as he released an exasperated sigh.

"That time of year again, is it?" he muttered, unimpressed. Without waiting for a reply, he reached over and stabbed the buttons. "There. Twelve, three, thirty."

"Is that the time?"

"The program," he said with an even weightier sigh, and as though explaining to a child, he said, "Twelve incline, three miles per hour, thirty minutes. Good for fat burning. It's easy."

Claire lurched forward as the treadmill ramped to a near-vertical incline. She gripped the handrails, concentrating on not toppling over—so much for warming up.

"Swing your arms," he said in a less harsh tone. "Helps with momentum. Only hold on if you must."

"O-oh, thank you," Claire said, trying to hide her wheezing. "I know your face, don't I?"

Tristan squinted at her and shook his head without needing to think.

"I saw you the other day," she continued. "At that giant Christmas pudding tent. Never forget a face."

Tristan blinked but otherwise kept his eyes trained ahead. "Oh. Yes, I was there. Just business."

"Ah, so you're in the restaurant business?" Claire asked innocently, despite knowing the answer. "Any other giant puddings on the horizon?"

"No." He looked her up and down again. "And I've got a few fingers in a few pies around town. Restaurants, pubs, shops..."

"Like an investor?"

"Not *like* an investor. I *am* an investor." Rolling his eyes, she could only imagine what he thought of her playing dumb, but it was getting information. "If it makes me money, I'll give it money."

"Thought about investing in The Park Inn? That place seems to be on the up and up."

"Only thanks to *moi*," he said, lips pricking into a smile. "Bought a controlling stake from the brewery. *I'm* the one who suggested they overhaul the menu and finally bring fine dining to this place. About time there was somewhere quality to eat." He cracked his neck, speeding his treadmill back up to a jog. "I poached their chef from a top London restaurant. I heard about him through a gym buddy who said *his* friend had trained at a top London restaurant and was ready for a new challenge."

"Would that chef be Marco?"

"It would."

"I'm sorry for your loss."

"Right." He punched the speed up another notch. "Terrible shame."

"Shame." Claire nodded along, her lungs burning. "That rec-ord attempt must have c-cost a pretty penny."

Tristan looked pleased at the implied compliment about his wealth. "I provided the financing for it, yes. That pudding was Marco's idea for drumming up publicity. He promised it would be good for profits for the pub. Pulled up some old articles of all the publicity the last pudding got that old codger for his restaurant back in the day." He snorted. "Should have known better than to trust that *weasel*."

Inclining forward to stretch her tight calves, Claire asked, "Doesn't sound like you were friends?"

"*Friends*? Marco didn't have friends," he grunted. "Marco was an arrogant, opportunistic so-and-so. I gave him a sizable loan to cover expenses based on projected earnings, but he squandered away the money on himself.

A lavish holiday with his girlfriend, paying off rent arrears he'd built up since moving to Northash. Charged all the new equipment and ingredients to the pub, shafting me twice. Should have cut ties earlier, but you know what they say about hindsight... should have listened to that old codger."

"Would that 'old codger' be Victor?"

"That's the fella," he agreed, rolling his eyes. "Warned Marco, getting to the tonne weight wouldn't be easy. Even with his guidance, Marco didn't break the record. So much for positive publicity, right?"

"R-right." Claire smiled, mulling over the information as she panted for breath. "Victor was guiding Marco?"

"Unofficially. Between us, I think Victor was jealous the giant plum pudding spotlight had shifted away from him..." He trailed off, glancing at his watch. "Well, enough chatter. I have to run—I'm meeting the new head chef at The Park Inn later. Need to lay down some rules for the kitchen so I don't have a repeat of Marco's reign."

"New head chef already?" Claire asked. "Marco's only been gone two days."

"We have a reputation to save." He slapped the stop button, and the treadmill ground to a halt. He put his feet to the side and took one deep breath, as though he'd only been on a light walk. "It's his sous-chef. He knows the place inside-out already. Easy transition."

"Best of luck with everything," Claire offered as Tristan wiped his machine down. "See you around."

With a curt nod, Tristan strutted off towards the showers. Claire slammed her hand on the treadmill stop button when he was out of sight. As the machine ground to a halt, she doubled over wheezing. Ryan appeared at her side, eyebrows raised as a woman claimed Tristan's treadmill and set off at the speed of a gazelle chasing after a fat Christmas turkey.

"Nine minutes? Not a bad start," he offered, handing her a towel and a water bottle. "I've seen people do less."

Claire gulped the water. "Turns out... I'm even less... fit... than I thought," she panted, wiping sweat from her brow. "Maybe next time."

"Did you at least get anything useful from Tristan?"

"Grant has already taken Marco's old job, which isn't looking good for him," she said, wiping her face with a towel as she watched Tristan chatting to someone by the lockers. "Tristan said a gym buddy told him about Marco. A friend of Marco's. I'd bet that was Grant, too. Does he come in here? A bald man who's always screaming at The Park Inn?"

Ryan nodded. "Grant's a member here. He always comes to my boxercise classes."

"Right. You told me that before. I don't think Grant was honest about his relationship with Marco."

After returning the sweat-soaked gym clothes, Claire

headed straight for her candle shop, still tingling with adrenaline. She burst through the door to find Damon bagging candles at the counter.

"Back so soon?" he asked with surprise. "Are you alright? You're sweating like it's summer out there."

"Two things you're never going to believe," she said in a low voice, rubbing at her sore thighs. "I've already spoken to *three* suspects and might have *accidentally* joined the gym."

"The *gym*?" came a delighted voice behind her. Claire spun to find her mother scanning the candles on sale, clutching her heart. "Oh, Claire! I've never been prouder. Suppose this could be a 'congratulations' present?" She handed out a bag before announcing, "Had that banner printed! Grab a ladder, and we'll get it put up. My little girl, finally getting fit!"

Claire cringed behind her smile, wondering which would be trickier—solving Marco's murder in the mix of the plum pudding mess or explaining her gym ruse to her mother.

CHAPTER EIGHT

*A*fter a hectic first day of The Sale at the shop, Claire and Damon finally flipped the 'Open' sign to 'Closed' as dusk settled over the village square. She sighed, resting her forehead against the icy glass in the door. December was always their busiest month, but the holiday crowds seemed even more agitated than usual.

"I don't know about you, but I'm ready to put my feet up with a cup of cocoa," Damon said, stretching his arms above his head.

Claire yawned as she locked the door. "And then I'm ready to sleep for a week. However, homebrew at the pub sounds perfect right about now. And maybe even another Christmas dinner."

"You've got to," Damon agreed. "Boxing Day is basically Christmas: Part Two."

"Electric Boogaloo?" Claire's next yawn turned into a laugh and then a groan as she stepped into the road to look up at the sign. "I do wish my mother would have phoned before she got the banner printed. 'Everything MUST Go' sounds like a closing down sale."

"Closing down? After today's takings, you'll be opening a second shop next year. New Year's resolution?"

"My New Year's resolution is to *not* use my new gym membership."

"I'll not use it with you." He winked, beckoning Claire to the glow of his phone as he stepped into the road. "Sally sent this. Looks like she's having fun without me."

He showed her a selfie of Sally on a ski slope, grinning behind her goggles, along with her mother and two young daughters.

"Can't believe she finds that fun," Claire said, linking arms as they crossed the road towards the winding down market. "How are things going with Sally, anyway? Apart from the forced ski trips, of course."

"Great, actually. She paid for my passes to all my sci-fi conventions next year for Christmas." His eyes softened. "And I know she doesn't know why I find that fun. I dragged her along to a couple over the summer, and I've never seen someone yawn so much." He craned his neck to stare into her open mouth. "Until today, that is."

"Late night. But that's so lovely to hear." She gave his arm an affectionate squeeze. "You two are surprisingly perfect together. The estate agent and the nerd."

"Sounds like a *Doctor Who* title."

"One track mind, Damon." They came to a stop outside The Hesketh Arms. "Fancy joining Ryan and me for dinner? My treat. You deserve it after covering for me today."

"I'll leave you two lovebirds to it," he said, checking his watch. "I should already be logged on. *Dawn Ship 2* tournament starts in three minutes. See you tomorrow, boss."

Damon hurried past the empty stall where her candles had been—she'd decided against opening after everything—and across the road towards his flat above Marley's Café. She glanced back at the giant pudding tent as she passed, its sides still cordoned off with police tape.

When Claire entered the pub's warmth, her eyes landed on Ryan waiting at their usual corner, and her heart lifted at the sight of him waving her over, two halves of homebrew already on the table.

"Got your usual," Ryan said as Claire unwound her scarf and jacket. "Although after all that Baileys yesterday, I didn't think the full pint would be a good idea."

Draping her coat over the chair's back, Claire scanned the pub, pausing on Elena. Nestled in an armchair by the fire, Elena's animated and intense discussion with someone on the armchair opposite captured Claire's attention.

"Did you notice who's with that woman by the fire?"

Ryan, engrossed in the menu, shook his head. "Been mulling over another Christmas dinner or this cheese and cranberry pie with buttermilk mash."

"The pie sounds tempting," Claire responded, her gaze still fixed on Elena. "You stay here. I'll order."

At the bar, Claire put in their food order with Theresa, and while she was in the kitchen, Claire tried to get a better look at Elena's companion. She saw the fire reflecting off the side of a bald head.

"Do you know who that woman in the armchair by the fire is? The one with the long dark hair?"

Theresa craned her neck for a better look. "Oh, that's Elena. She came in here nearly daily with her man some months back."

"Marco?"

"The dead chef?" Theresa shook her head. "That man she's with now. They were all snug as two bugs in a rug, but it doesn't seem so cosy today." She leaned in, dropping her voice. "They've been bickering ever since they got here. Lover's quarrel, I reckon."

Claire wanted to talk to Theresa and Malcolm about the day of the stabbing, but she was too intrigued by Elena to miss out. With her order placed, she set off towards the bathroom. She slowed as she passed the armchairs by the fire, her ears tuning into the heated conversation.

"There's *no* going back, not after this," Elena insisted. "I'm going to tell the police everything. I *need* to."

"*No!*" the bald man replied, and Claire instantly recognised the voice as Grant's. "Don't be stupid, Elena. If you tell them, they're going to ruin *everything*. I'm finally getting what I deserve."

Not wanting to risk being noticed, Claire ducked into the bathroom. Standing at the sink, she turned on the tap, letting the water cascade over her hands. Her calm reflection in the mirror betrayed her racing thoughts.

No going back?

Finally getting what he deserved?

It didn't sound good.

The abrupt whoosh of a toilet flushing made Claire jump. She glanced up to see Leslie Clark exiting the stall, shooting her a frosty look before taking the sink furthest away. Claire hadn't seen Leslie since Granny Greta had given her a verbal smack-down when she'd wrapped her nails around Claire's arm.

In the mirror, Leslie's glare seemed to bore right through Claire. After a terse silence, she finally spoke.

"I believe I owe you an apology for the other day in the market." She scrubbed at her hands. "I was rather short with you after a testing phone call. My father can be quite... demanding. Put me in the *worst* mood."

Claire sensed an opening—a chance to address the hatred from Leslie losing her job to Marco.

"No need to apologise. Marco taking over your position at the pub must have been difficult."

At the mention of Marco, Leslie bristled, pink rising in her cheeks. She scrubbed her hands harder, the hot tap steaming against her skin.

"I was unfairly dismissed from The Park Inn during a regime change," she snapped. "I intend to pursue the matter legally." Twisting off the tap, she snatched a pile of paper towels and added, "Perhaps I'll use those proceeds to fund my record attempt. After all, if anyone in this village *deserves* that plum pudding glory, it's *me*." Chin lifted, and she headed for the door. "It's *my* destiny. It's in *my* blood. Marco was a nobody."

The oddly specific declaration nagged at Claire even after Leslie's departure. In her blood? Heart racing, Claire hurried back to Ryan, their cheese and cranberry pies waiting on their table.

"You won't believe what I just overheard," Claire whispered after scanning for eavesdroppers. She quickly relayed the heated exchange between Elena and Grant. "Elena wants to go to the police about something, but Grant is trying to stop her. They're hiding something."

Ryan nodded as he cut into his pie, the gooey cheese spilling out. "Definitely suspicious. Sounds like something the police *should* hear about."

"Exactly. But there's more." Claire leaned in further. "I just had a cryptic chat with Leslie Clark in the loo. I think... I think she might be Victor's daughter?"

"Victor, as in the plum pudding record holder?"

Claire gave a definite nod. "It makes sense. She said the record was in *her* blood. That it was *her* destiny. Her connection to Victor would explain some of the hate beyond Marco for stealing her job."

"Hmm." He chewed for a moment, fanning his hot mouth. "Do you think it's important?"

Claire shook her head in disbelief as she scooped up some creamy mashed potato. "I'm not sure. Strange connection."

Ryan smiled warmly and lifted his glass. "Well, here's to your uncanny talent for being in the right place to uncover secrets. And for piecing together this mystery when no one else can."

Heart swelling with gratitude, Claire clinked her glass to his and took a long sip of the comforting homebrew. She hoped Ryan was right—her knack for stumbling upon clues would ultimately unravel the truth behind Marco's untimely end.

"Ready to go?" Ryan asked once their table had been cleared. "Need to pick the kids up from Em's boat."

"Wait for me outside," Claire said. "Something I need to do first."

Malcolm leaned across the worn oak bar, laughing

with a customer over a pint. Nearby, Theresa beamed, tucking a bill into the bulging tip jar.

Claire approached, biting her lip. "Hello, Theresa, Malcolm. Do you... might I have a quick word?"

"What can we do for you, love?" Malcolm greeted warmly, gesturing her nearer. But as she shifted in front of them, their smiles faded.

"This isn't easy for me to bring up." Claire met their eyes, seeing confusion swirling in Theresa's gaze and dawning offence in Malcolm's. "But... where were you both when Marco was... when I heard that scream and ran outside?"

Theresa froze, rag hovering over a half-cleaned glass. Malcolm stiffened, grip tightening around his pint glass.

"Why do you want to know?" he demanded.

Claire raised her palms. "I'm trying to find out who killed Marco. You both had tensions with him over the competition he brought..."

Malcolm slammed down his glass, the thud turning heads. "You think *we* killed him? That's preposterous! Marco may have been competition, but we'd never resort to... to..." He struggled to form words, face reddening.

"Sweetheart, however ugly things got between the pubs, we would never do what you suggest." Theresa rested a trembling hand over Claire's. "The Hesketh is our family, our livelihood. We could never jeopardise that."

"I'm sorry, I had to ask to..."

"The *nerve*, after all the pints we've pulled you!" Malcolm's lips twisted into a snarl. "Get out, now!"

"Malcolm..." Theresa shot him a glare.

"Don't you 'Malcolm' me! She all but accused us of being cold-blooded killers!"

Cheeks mottling with rage, he gestured sharply towards the door. As customers turned to stare, Theresa whispered soothingly to Malcolm. At last, he jerked his head toward the back.

"Fine," Malcolm called to Claire as she set off to the door. "If you *must* know, I was talking to Drunken Pete in the beer garden out back when Marco was attacked. We'd been there awhile. He can vouch I never left his sight."

Nodding gratefully, Claire hurried out the back entrance into the small, snow-dusted beer garden backing onto the canal. It was empty, save for a few overturned chairs. Her heart sank. She whirled back inside, shivering.

"Pete isn't there."

Malcolm threw up his hands, but Theresa touched his arm gently.

"Love, Pete leaves when the weather dips. You know that." Theresa turned to Claire, eyes crinkling. "Perhaps it's time to let the police handle things?"

Nodding in concession, Claire ducked out the front entrance. She sighed, breath frosting the winter air. One more thread to unravel in the tangled web of Marco's murder.

"Was that Malcolm I heard shouting?" Ryan asked.

"Nothing," Claire whispered, looping her arm tight around his. "I hope."

She'd wanted to rule Malcolm out, but his outburst only made Claire suspect him more.

———

CLAIRE DESCENDED THE NARROW STAIRS INTO RYAN'S makeshift art studio in the cellar of his cottage. She inhaled the familiar scents of oil paints and turpentine mingling with the earthy must of the underground room. Ryan stood before a large canvas propped on an easel, palette in hand. Strokes of vivid purple brought Claire's candle shop to life, the giant papier mâché plum in the window taking shape.

"That plum looks so real I want to reach out and squeeze it," Claire said.

"Still needs some work, but I'm getting there." He dabbed more purple onto the canvas. "How are you getting on with the case? Any progress?"

Claire perched on a stool, shoulders slumping. "Honestly, I feel like I'm just going around in circles. Especially after upsetting Malcolm and Theresa by questioning their innocence." She shook her head. "I'm lost in the mix of suspects and motives." She nodded at the painting. "This is excellent work, Ryan. You captured all the little details perfectly."

Ryan shrugged, brushing off the compliment. "Just a little something to pass the time."

"Speaking of your art, I sold more of your Christmas cards today. You'd better start thinking about which piece you'll submit to the gallery."

"Oh, I don't know..."

Claire stood before Ryan could brush her off again, a playful smile curving her lips. She wrapped her arms around his neck, melting against him. "I know the perfect inspiration."

She drew him into a tender kiss. After a moment, Ryan responded, his arms encircling her as the cellar vanished. Claire cherished the blissful escape, the lingering homebrew taste on Ryan's lips.

All too soon, the patter of footsteps sounded on the stairs, followed by Hugo's voice shouting, "*Daaad*, we're bored!"

They parted with a rueful chuckle. Ryan called up, "Be right there!" To Claire, he said, "Guess we'd better go entertain them before they destroy the house out of boredom."

Claire smoothed his ruffled hair. "Why don't we all go out for a fun evening? My treat. We could go bowling and catch a film. Take advantage of the holidays while they're off school."

Ryan's eyes lit up. "Brilliant idea. Kids will love it." He squeezed her hand. "Thank you, Claire. You always know how to cheer me up."

Arm-in-arm, they started up the narrow stairs. Claire treasured these moments with her chosen family amid the chaos and uncertainty. She could face whatever lay ahead if she had them by her side. And she hoped after a game of bowling, she'd start seeing things a little clearer.

CHAPTER NINE

*T*he low winter sun had yet to peek over the rooftops of Northash as Claire hurried around the corner towards Marley's Café the next morning. Frost sparkled on the cobbles underfoot, remnants of the light snowfall that had dusted the village overnight. She pulled her scarf tighter against the chill, breathing warmth into her cupped palms before pushing open the café door.

The smell of freshly brewed coffee and the sound of sizzling greeted her. Despite the early hour, the small space was already humming with customers vying for a table. Claire joined the queue as she glanced around the busy café, catching snippets of conversation from early risers reading their newspapers over tea and toast. Her gaze settled on a familiar face seated with a group of women by the window—Granny Greta.

Claire smiled, wishing she'd inherited her gran's early riser gene. Even after years of factory work and running her shop, Claire didn't roll out of bed without a fight most mornings, though, this morning, she'd awoken slumped on the sofa to Domino kneading at her chest, the cheering from winning all three rounds of bowling still echoing in her ears. Around her gran, a gaggle of silver-haired friends were chatting over a shared teapot.

"Morning, Marley. Two sausage sandwiches on sourdough rolls, please. Extra ketchup on both."

Claire handed over a crumpled five-pound note, and while Marley got to work assembling her order, she edged closer to Granny Greta's table, hoping to overhear their conversation. She caught something about the good old days of Northash as she crept nearer.

"It's such a shame how things have changed around here," one woman tutted into her teacup. "We used to have so many options. What now? The chippy, this place where everything is *vegan*, and two pubs?"

"And The Park Inn's new menu is fine, but remember that nice Italian we used to have around the corner?"

Granny Greta gave an adamant nod. "Too right, Beatrice. And since old Victor's restaurant shut down, the food scene around here has never been the same. The kids won't even know."

Claire must have been one of the 'kids' because she didn't remember Northash ever having much of a 'food scene'. She moved closer at the mention of Victor Michaels. She leaned against the wall watching the silent morning TV, keeping her back to the women as if waiting for her food, angling her head to better catch their words over the din of the café.

"Victor's was the pride of Northash back in its heyday," another woman said with a sigh. "Nowhere could match those exquisite sauces and perfect soufflés."

"Don't forget that legendary plum pudding," Beatrice added. "Folks used to flock from miles around every Christmas just for a taste, even before he went and made the history books. Doubt Marco's would have compared. Victor was so particular about getting the *perfect* plums. They had to be *Damson* plums imported, especially from Kent. He'd send his staff driving halfway across the country to collect them."

"Oh yes, I remember those damned Damsons!" Greta cried, mid-slurp of her tea. "When I was waitressing there, he was utterly obsessed with tracking down every Damson plum to ensure that pudding was flawless. No other plum would do. Used to drive the kitchen staff mad. Everybody swore they couldn't taste the difference, but Victor was *Victor*."

"Gran, I didn't know you worked for Victor

Michaels?" Claire said, stepping forward. "When was that?"

Granny Greta's eyes crinkled warmly at her granddaughter. "Oh, must have been...mid-eighties?" She pursed her lips, reminiscing. "A few years before he made that giant pudding. Only a few hours here and there. More to make ends meet than a real job."

"What was Victor like to work for?" Claire asked.

"*Insufferable!*" Granny Greta declared with a snort. "Never met a man so obsessed with *perfection*. He'd hover over our shoulders, watching everything, snapping if a fork was out of place. Had no patience at all."

"I have no idea how Wendy put up with him," Beatrice added, half under her breath. "She was as placid as a pond, though I suppose opposites attract."

"Wendy?" Claire asked.

"Victor ended up marrying his sous-chef, Wendy," Greta said. "Lovely woman she was. I could tell he had eyes for her when I worked there, but I don't think she noticed him like that. Not until he broke that record."

"People used to say she only went with him for the fame." Beatrice rolled her eyes as she topped up her tea. "Which, if you knew Wendy, was ridiculous. I always thought she fell in love with his passion. We were *all* behind him in '87. Northash had never had so much attention until then."

"Wendy passed away a few years back." Greta lifted

her teacup to the ceiling. "Cancer. Poor woman. I bet it tore Victor apart."

Folding her arms, Claire asked, "Did Victor and Wendy have a daughter by any chance?"

"Why yes, they *did*!" piped up Eugene from behind the counter. "I remember a little girl always running around the restaurant in the final few years."

"A little girl called Leslie, by any chance?" Claire asked.

"That's it!" Beatrice said. "Leslie Michaels."

"I think it's Leslie Clark these days," Claire corrected, leaning closer to her gran. "She's the one who grabbed my arm in the market the other day."

"*That* was Victor's little one?" Greta almost choked on her tea. "She was always such a sweet girl. I wonder where it all went wrong."

"She apologised," Claire said with a slight shrug. "She was stressed because her dad kept calling her, demanding something of her."

Greta's eyebrows shot up. "Did he now?"

"I saw her lingering around the tent. I wonder if Victor wanted her to spy for him or gather information?"

"Demanding that she sunk a blade into Marco's back, by any chance?"

"Oh, Greta, you're *wicked*!" Beatrice gasped with a chuckle. "Not that she'd need much encouragement. You must have heard how much she lost her temper when she found out she was to be replaced by Marco?"

"I was in the pub then!" Eugene exclaimed, hurrying around the counter. "Blew her top off. Said she'd ruined Marco."

"She was insistent the record attempt was her birthright, so maybe he wanted her to interfere or stop Marco somehow?" Claire suggested, nibbling her lip as she cast her eyes to the window as more snow fluttered down.

"Wouldn't surprise me with Victor," Greta whispered. "A control freak, if ever I've met one, always had to control every detail. It's part of the reason I left. Oh, good morning, Damon."

Claire turned to see Damon walking from the direction of the door leading to his flat above the café, still half asleep by the looks of things. He was technically ten minutes late, but so was Claire. Marley called her name and handed over their breakfast rolls. She passed one to Damon as they left the café.

"Stranger things get stranger," she told him as she wrapped her fingers around the warm brown bag. "Victor used a *specific* plum variety. Damson, and I saw that same plum written in the recipe for Marco's attempt."

"Damsons?" Damon wrinkled his nose. "They're tiny and kinda gross. Tart."

"Makes sense for a plum pudding," she said. "But it's not the plum that's important. It can't be a coincidence that Marco used the same specific plum, right? Tristan suggested Victor was guiding Marco." She met Damon's curious gaze. "Do you think it's suspicious Victor would *willingly* help Marco try to beat his record?"

"I wouldn't help anyone beat my Pac-Man score at that arcade out of town. Still hasn't been touched for eleven years," Damon replied through a mouthful of food as they weaved through the market. "Would never know these sausages were vegan, would you?" Fanning his steaming mouth, he added, "You did say you saw Marco dragging Victor out of the tent on Christmas Eve, and he was lingering around before Marco was stabbed. You think Victor was trying to help Marco?"

"Or hinder?" Claire suggested, fishing the shop keys from her pocket as they reached the door. "Even if he hadn't been stabbed, Marco didn't beat Victor's record, did he? His pudding weighed less."

"Are you suggesting Victor sabotaged the attempt somehow?"

"I'm not sure, but it seems fishy, right?" Twisting the key in the lock, she glanced back at the white tent. "Another strange thing for the list of strange things."

Before she could push open the door, she caught sight of Granny Greta hurrying around the corner with Spud in tow. She caught up and gave Claire an affectionate pinch on the cheek.

"I've got faith you'll have this whole mess sorted soon enough." She leaned in with a tut and said, "Certainly before that fool, Detective Ramsbottom. He was in the café ten minutes before you and didn't give a toffee about the case. More interested in talking about his breakfast."

Claire laughed. "Well, I am rather invested in this breakfast roll."

"I'll let you know if I remember anything else about Victor," Granny Greta offered, patting Claire's cheek. "Oh, and before I forget. I overheard the strangest conversation between Malcolm and Theresa the night before Marco's death at the pub. They were muttering about that chef Marco between themselves."

Claire's ears perked up. "Oh? What about?"

"Going on about how he's stealing all their business with his flashy new pub makeover and menu. Worried they'll have to shut up shop before long." Greta leaned in, dropping her voice. "And then Theresa said they ought to take *drastic measures*."

"Drastic measures?" Claire repeated.

"Plant something dodgy in that kitchen tent to get Marco reported. Shut him down for a while until things blow over, which shocked me to no end. Not like them at all." Greta checked her watch. "Well, must dash. But do keep an eye on those two. Desperate people and all... You've got this, Claire. We're all behind you."

With an air kiss, Greta shuffled off towards the park, Spud panting at her heels. Claire stared after her gran, wondering what it could all mean.

"Could those drastic measures have ended up being the knife in Marco's back?" Damon wondered aloud.

"Whatever they intended, this confirms they were willing to go to concerning lengths to eliminate the competition Marco posed. I just hope I'm wrong about them..."

Claire unlocked the shop, and while Damon flicked on the lights and heating, she nibbled at her sandwich, deep in thought.

"What's got you smiling?" Damon asked as he restocked the frosted plum jars in the centre. "Fun night with Ryan? I saw those pictures from bowling. Well done on your triple win."

"Thank you." She offered a bow, licking the last of the ketchup from her lips. "And I'm smiling because I finally feel like I'm getting somewhere with this case. I need to talk with Theresa and Malcolm again, but before then, let's have an extended lunch break later. I heard The Park Inn has another new head chef, and I'm eager to sample what they can do."

CHAPTER TEN

$\mathcal{C}$laire's mouth watered as she awaited her lunch order at The Park Inn, tucked in a corner booth perfect for people-watching. The savoury aromas wafting from the kitchen promised another masterpiece from the new head chef, while the people at the surrounding tables were eating with lid-fluttering bliss.

While Damon studied the menu that they'd already ordered from, Claire's eyes settled on a familiar face seated alone near the fireplace where the pool table used to stand. Leslie Clark nursed a glass of red wine, glancing at her watch between sips.

She leaned towards Damon, speaking low. "Looks like Leslie might be waiting for her father, Victor. Maybe I'll go over and say hello. Might finally be my chance to chat with him."

"Good thinking," Damon replied, flipping the menu to the desserts. "Get the full suspects set, and you might even catch them in the act of discussing how they got away with murder."

The father and the daughter duo might not have worked together to bring forth Marco's downfall, but it was an interesting theory. She sipped her beer, wishing it was a pint of Hesketh Homebrew. And the rest of the pub, for that matter. The Hesketh looked like a cosy sitting room filled with local paintings and framed memories perfect for Northash; The Park Inn's tasteful—and soulless—décor could have been plucked from any town anywhere in the country.

Before Claire could finish counting how many tables had been crammed in narrow rows to turn the once quiet pub into a bustling restaurant, their young waiter brought out their plates.

"As nice as it looks," Damon whispered, glancing at his plate, "for what we paid, where's the rest? It's all very 'blob and drizzle.'"

"That's fine dining for you."

"I'll take a fine mountain of food from the Hesketh for three pounds less any day of the week." He sliced his buttery turkey and dipped it in the smear of cranberry sauce around the edge before forking on the lone sprout. It went into his mouth, and he pulled the same face he had when she'd offered him her third draft of the new frosted plum scent. "Okay, I'll hand it to their new head chef. Delicious. Better than my mum's."

"Mine too," Claire said, slicing the crispy yet fluffy roast potato in two. "Merry Christmas: Part Three."

They finished their lunch silently, too busy enjoying the delicate flavours and textures. Claire cast her gaze in Leslie's direction a few times as she sipped and clock-watched, but there was still no sign of her guest. When Claire pushed the plate away and reached for the menu to scan the desserts, Damon's phone pinged.

"Probably another ski slope selfie from Sally. At this rate, she'll have sent an album's worth by the time she gets back," he said, digging his phone out of his jeans. "Think she's trying to make me jealous that I'm missing out."

"While you reply," she said, gathering their two plates, "I might see if I can pass our compliments onto the new chef… in person."

With her empty plates in hand, Claire approached one of the young servers engrossed in clearing a nearby table. She looked up as she neared, her worn expression that of someone who'd worked far too much over Christmas.

"Excuse me, this was delicious," she said, to which the girl sighed. "I just wanted to pass my compliments on to the chef, but I can see you're busy, so I wouldn't mind doing it myself."

The waiter offered a hesitant smile, glancing towards

the kitchen noise. She shrugged a gesture that Claire took as approval. With a grateful nod, she made her way towards the kitchen.

She hadn't expected it to be so easy.

Pushing on the swinging door, she poked her head through the doorway, and the apparent absence of shouting struck her. During his stint as Marco's sous-chef, Grant's fiery temper often disrupted the dining room, with his outbursts echoing through the doors. A focused intensity filled the kitchen as Grant and his staff worked in harmony at their stations, with no trace of the dramatic tantrums Claire had overheard during her previous visit.

Perhaps with Marco gone, Grant was finally in his element as head chef. Or maybe the pressure of the investigation had doused his volatile temper. In either case, the cannon was no longer firing after his promotion.

"*Service!*" Grant called in her direction in a level tone, patting a brass bell on the pass. The waiter swept in to collect the prepared dishes around Claire as she stood there like a spare part. He glanced up, and his eyes narrowed. "*You...*"

"Grant, I—"

"Customers can't be back here," he snapped, looking past her as the waiter scurried out. "Who said you could come back here?"

Claire offered her most placating smile, but it only furrowed Grant's brows more. "I didn't mean to intrude. I just wanted to let you know this was the best Christmas dinner I've ever eaten. You should have seen my mum's roast potatoes this year. Like lumps of coal."

Grant's stern expression didn't waver at Claire's attempt at softening him. He crossed his burly arms, white chef's jacket pulled taut. "Anything else?"

Claire almost put the plates down and hurried out from his stare alone, but she stiffened her spine. She rested the plates against her front, rocking back on her heels as she looked around the kitchen.

"Heard you were promoted?" she pointed out. "I suppose when one head chef falls, another must rise…"

With a resigned sigh, Grant declared everyone should take a five-minute break and waved his staff away. Claire settled onto a stool beside the expansive metal prep surface while Grant stood opposite, his imposing frame towering over her.

"Alright, out with it," he demanded, grabbing an onion and a sharp knife. "The sooner you spit out what you've got to say, the sooner you can get out of my kitchen."

Claire took a deep breath before revealing what she suspected to be the truth.

"Last time we spoke, I told you about what my source overheard when you quit this place," she started. "About how you claimed you were the mastermind behind

Marco's ideas? After tasting your food today, I think you were being honest then. I wouldn't be surprised if *you* designed his menu here at The Park Inn before his death. I think you got him the job here, too."

Grant froze mid-slice, the knife hovering over the onions on his cutting board. He glanced up, lowering the knife and rubbing his stubbly jaw. "What makes you so sure?"

"Because I know you and Tristan are gym buddies," she revealed, hiding her smile at his surprised, widening eyes. "I believe you were the one who recommended Marco for the head chef position."

Grant shrugged as if to say, 'What of it?' as he diced the onion at lightning speed. He sniffed, his eyes watering.

"Alright, you got me," he admitted after a stretch of rhythmic chopping. "Marco and I went to culinary school together before he got whisked away to some fancy London restaurant. One viral video of him making a Wellington boot-shaped beef Wellington, and suddenly, Marco was destined to become the next *big thing*."

"I think I might have seen that."

"*Everyone* saw it." Grant's dicing grew more forceful as he vented his frustration. "Charismatic, good-looking Marco. Of course, he got the easy ride to fame and fortune. Image is everything in the high-end culinary world these days. They want you to be a model, a chef, an influencer… it's not why I got into this game."

He clicked on the gas stove with a burst of flames. After drizzling oil into a sizzling pan, Grant tossed in the onions.

"Why did you get into this game?"

"For the cooking." He sent the onions to the edge of the pan before tossing them back to the middle with a flick of his wrist. "Grew up learning from my Nan. Pie and mash, fish and chips, Sheppard's pie… I could make the lot before I got to secondary school. It's all I wanted to do."

"Then I can't imagine it was easy watching your friend get everything handed to him on a plate."

"What do *you* think?" he grunted. "Never mind that he was an average cook."

"But you *did* recommend Marco for the head chef job here?" she pushed. "Why suggest him for the opportunity if you resented his success?"

Grant's tossing slowed as he considered his response. "I only told Tristan about Marco because he fits what Tristan wanted to revamp this place. He knew the food was one thing, but a small place like this needed someone likeable. Someone who could turn on the charm when needed. It's theatre." He drizzled in more oil, and the flames seared up the sides. "I was happy to see the back of Marco when he was whisked away, but he called me one night out of the blue. He was drunk, and we hadn't talked in years. He was in tears about losing his job. They saw through him in the end. He was desperate to move on to some new place that hadn't caught onto him yet, and we owed me a favour."

"A favour?"

With a heavy sigh, Grant set down the pan and looked up to face her. "That viral video that launched his career? It was *my* idea, and I said it as a joke. People need gimmicks, but I only care about the food being the best it can be. Nobody cared through the screen that his beef was as chewy as leather and his Yorkshire pudding was brittle. If I brought Marco back here to be head chef, he'd need a sous-chef he could hide behind."

"And that was you?"

"Beat breaking my back at that motorway service station carvery for the rest of my life." He returned to the stove, where the onions started caramelising, filling the kitchen with their sweet aroma. "It was fine being the sous-chef at first. I got to come up with new ideas and cook real food. But the guy wouldn't stop stealing *my* ideas. Never gave credit where it was due."

Claire nodded. "So, the whole new menu *was* your creation?"

"All of it. I waited for Marco to toss me a bone, but it never came." Grant vigorously tossed the darkening onions, sending some falling to smoulder in the flames.

"That plum pudding stunt? *I* told Marco about that. My nan used to talk about it all the time when I was a kid. She gave me my love of cooking, and those stories... that memory is sacred to *me*, but Marco snatched it up without a thought. He announced he would break the record to the whole pub an hour after I brought it up."

"Grant, I'm sorry that's—"

"And the more he learned about Victor Michaels' glory days," he steamed ahead, his lips snarling as more onions joined the crispy runaways, "the more Marco was convinced he could replicate it. A huge tonne-weight gimmick to hide the fact that he's not a very good chef!"

With a final forceful stir, Grant scraped the deeply caramelised onions into a waiting bowl, and a wave of sympathy washed over Claire. She couldn't help but draw parallels to her own experiences. Not so long ago, there was a time when her vanilla bean formula, the one she had meticulously crafted during her days at the candle factory on the hill, was stolen. The memory of that betrayal still stung whenever she thought about it. It had been more than just a formula; it was a piece of her, her creativity and hard work, snatched from her little black book by her former boss; she'd met a sticky end like Marco, too.

Still, Grant's betrayal was more profound than that. What if the betrayal had come from someone closer? Claire couldn't help but wonder how she would have felt if Damon had been the one to steal her formula. The mere thought sent a shiver down her spine.

Grant's temper made sense, but Claire couldn't lose sight of why she was there.

A man had been murdered.

A man Grant had several reasons to want out of the way.

Claire inhaled, ready to share her last sizzling scrap of information.

"It wasn't just your ideas and family stories Marco stole," she exhaled. "Elena was *your* girlfriend before she and Marco got together."

He froze, stare trained on the onions.

"That's why she ran out without talking to you after seeing you in the tent," Claire continued. "And I saw you two together at the pub the other day. Close… arguing…"

Grant remained silent for a long moment. "What of it? Elena and I dated for a few years before Marco came along. Doesn't matter now. Marco's gone, and he can't take anything more from me."

He turned away, busying himself with cleaning up his station. The conversation could have ended there, but Claire had come this far. She cleared her throat and he cast a glare over his shoulder.

"I heard you and Elena in the pub," she pushed. "Elena wants to go to the police about something. To *confess* something. Something you'd rather keep secret. What was it you said? You'd finally got everything you deserved?" She hesitated, then whispered, "Something that might connect *you* to Marco's death?"

Grant froze, the empty pan still popping and cracking on the hob in the silence, and Claire held her breath, unsure if she'd crossed a line. He slammed a flat palm on the metal surface, his eyes ablaze with rage.

"I think you should go," he said, veins bulging on his forehead.

Claire slid off the stool but she stood her ground as Grant snatched up the knife, its edge flecked with onion skins. He pointed it sharply towards the exit.

"I'm not leaving until I have the truth," she said, summoning her courage as she followed the glinting knife waving in his hand. "It's understandable if you killed Marco after everything he took from you."

With a guttural roar, Grant slammed the knife through a fresh onion, slicing it in two. The knife jutted up from the chopping board, and Claire jumped back, heart in her throat as he rounded the counter, face twisted in fury.

"Get out!" He reached across and wrenched the knife from the board as she staggered back. "*Now!*"

Claire fled the kitchen, pulse hammering. She'd ignited Grant's simmering rage but was no closer to a confession. Still, she'd struck a nerve. She rushed back to Damon, still staring at his phone.

"You won't believe what's just happened," she breathed, pulse racing as she slid into her seat. "Grant just—"

"Neither will you," he cut in, turning the screen to show the inside of a hospital. "I just got a text from Sally. It turns out the skiing was too much for her mum. She's only gone and broken her hip!"

"That's... terrible," Claire said, still distracted and breathing heavily. Her wide eyes darted around the dining room, searching for Leslie. But Leslie wasn't there to meet her father. Instead, she was at the bar with Tristan, grinning about something.

"What unbelievable thing happened to you in that kitchen?" Damon asked.

Claire leaned in close, voice scarcely above a whisper. "Grant just threatened me... with a *knife*."

Before Damon could respond, a familiar thick mane of grey hair at the bar caught Claire's eye. It was Victor Michaels, nursing a pint alone. Claire took a calming breath and realised this was her chance to speak with him finally. She moved to claim the stool next to Victor when the bubbly pop of a cork pierced the steady hum of the dining room. Conversations quieted, and heads turned as Leslie gripped a bottle of champagne, giggling excitedly as the fizz spilt into a glass.

She tapped her glass with a spoon, drawing the full attention of the pub. Victor's gaze snapped up in surprise at the interruption. Around him, diners lowered their forks, glancing towards the gleeful woman with champagne.

"Thank you all for your attention," Leslie announced, beaming wide. "As some of you know, *I* was the chef here, at The Park Inn." Her smile faltered slightly. "That is, until, I was unfairly let go and replaced by Marco as head chef." She brightened again. "But due to recent *circumstances*, Tristan has generously offered me my old job back, and thanks to Tristan, I'm not only getting my old job back as the chef..."

"*Sous*-chef," Tristan interrupted.

"Yes, sous-chef," Leslie corrected with a tittering laugh. "On top of returning to the kitchen team here, I'll also be continuing what Marco couldn't. And in honour of my father—" She raised her glass to Victor "—I'll pick up Marco's torch, finish that giant plum pudding, and beat the record before the new year!"

Tepid applause rippled around the dining room as Leslie beamed. But the most significant reaction came from Victor himself. Squeezing his pint glass, it burst into shards of glass in his thick palm, cutting his hand. He rushed out of the pub without a word, leaving a trail of blood drops behind.

Shocked gasped swelled through the crowd, and Claire could only wonder what on earth had happened. Leslie back in the kitchen, Marco's plum pudding stunt back on... and Victor's violent reaction? Her head spun, trying to make sense of it all.

"Well, that was... *unexpected*?" Damon murmured. "What do you make of it?"

"Not sure," Claire admitted, staring at the bloody shards of glass in the beer puddle on the bar. "But I think we may have found our next lead. We need to speak with Victor and find out why he reacted like that to his daughter's announcement. You alright to open the shop up without me?" Squaring her shoulders, Claire turned to the door. "I think it's time I speak to Victor Michaels."

CHAPTER ELEVEN

*H*eart still pounding from the confrontation with Grant in the kitchen, Claire hurried after Victor's trail of blood drops staining the dusting of snow in the direction of the market. She couldn't shake the image of his hand clamped around the shattered pint glass, the crimson liquid seeping between his fingers. What had caused that reaction? She saw his hunched frame stumbling through the market stalls towards The Hesketh Arms.

"Victor, *wait!*" Claire called out, dodging shoppers examining hand-knitted scarves and carved wooden trinkets. "You should be going to the hospital."

But Victor didn't slow his pace, focused on his path to the pub. Claire huffed, quickening her steps over the cobblestones, breaking into a jog for the second time that week as raindrops began pelting down. The winter sky above was a gloomy grey blanket. Inside the pub, warmth and conversation beckoned as she caught the door before it slammed behind Victor. He ran straight for the gent's bathroom, the door sealing behind him.

Before she could consider following, a cheerful voice called out.

"Claire? Fancy seeing you here."

Claire turned to find Ryan seated at their usual corner table with Em, half-eaten salads between them. He flashed his familiar grin that never failed to lift her spirits.

"Drama at the *other* pub," Claire greeted, catching her breath. She cast a glance at the bathroom door Victor had disappeared behind. "And the one man I want to speak to has gone to the one place I can't."

Ryan and Em exchanged puzzled looks.

"Victor."

"The plum pudding champion?" Em clarified. "The whole village went plum pudding crazy that year. Funny that you've got your frosted plum display in your shop right now because when that used to be my mum's tearoom, she had plum-flavoured *everything* in the winter of 1987." She smiled at the fond memory before catching Claire's worried stare. "What happened at the other pub?"

Claire quickly relayed the scene she'd left at The Park Inn, from Leslie announcing her new sous-chef role and re-attempting Marco's record, followed by her father's glass-shattering reaction.

"That's quite strange," Ryan remarked. "Any idea why Victor responded so severely to the news? If anyone were going to break his record, surely he'd be happy for it to be his daughter?"

"That's exactly what I need to find out."

"I can try talking to him?" Ryan suggested, already pushing on the door. "See if I can get to the bottom of things? May open up more easily, man-to-man."

Claire sagged with relief. Trust Ryan to step in without hesitation. "Thank you, sidekick. Let's hope he isn't squeezing out through the window."

Ryan disappeared into the bathroom, leaving Claire to sink into an armchair by the fireplace. Bringing over her salad bowl, Em perched in the chair across from her, the crackling flames between them. Seated by the fire with Em, Claire hoped to steer the conversation towards something more illuminating.

"Em, you know everyone in town. Do you know Elena? She's a bit alternative, like you."

Em nodded, her expression thoughtful. "Elena? She *used* to come to my yoga classes. I haven't seen her in a while. Not since she and Grant split up. She wasn't the same after Grant left her."

Claire's eyebrows shot up in surprise. "Grant left

Elena? I'd assumed it had happened the other way around, especially after hearing about her and Marco."

Em shook her head. "No, it was *definitely* Grant who ended things. Elena confided in me about how hard she took it. 'Blindsided' was the word she used. And Marco? He swooped in soon after."

Claire mulled over this new piece of information as she stared into the dancing flames. The dynamics between Elena, Grant, and Marco were more complex than she had initially thought. What had Elena said sat in the same chair Em was in now?

"'There's *no* going back, not after this,'" Claire echoed. "I wonder if Elena was talking about getting back together with Grant? And the 'after this' being…"

"Grant murdering Marco?"

Claire shrugged, but she couldn't help but feel a tinge of unease, the image of Grant clutching the knife still vivid in her mind. Like whoever had stabbed Marco, he'd reached straight for a knife as his first rage-filled instinct.

"You alright, Claire? You seem a bit shaken up."

Claire forced a smile, not wanting to worry Em. "I'm fine, just a lot on my mind."

"Well, if you're looking for Elena, she works at the clothes shop next to the gallery down by Marley's. Might find her there." As Em stood, she reached across and clasped Claire's hands. "Remember, the universe doesn't throw anything at us that we can't handle. Amid the chaos, find your centre and trust your intuition. It's your internal compass and won't steer you wrong."

"Thanks, Em," Claire replied, grateful for the lead and the pick-me-up. "You always know how to cheer me up."

"Anytime." She winked. "And drop by the gym for a yoga session sometime. I heard you signed up from your mother. I don't think I've ever seen her so excited."

Before Claire could ponder the case further—and think of a way to let her mother down gently—Ryan emerged from the bathroom, tapping his phone in his palm.

"Managed to get a recording with Victor," he said, perching across from her. "Can you believe the guy smells like plums, too? I'm sure he had some in his pocket. He was surprisingly willing to talk, though his hand was bleeding quite badly. I helped pick the glass out and wrapped it in some toilet roll, which seemed to help, but he's refusing to get it looked at by a doctor."

"Can I…?"

He tossed her his phone. "You'll want to listen properly, but I think we've got a solid new lead. I need to get back to the gym before my lunch break ends, but I'll see you tonight at yours?"

"Thank you, Ryan, you're a star." Claire leaned over to plant a swift kiss on his cheek. A light blush rose on his face. "Of course. And bring the kids. I'm in the mood for family night."

Claire scrolled through his phone to play the recording as Ryan hurried out into the rain. She tensed as Victor's low, strained voice filled her ears.

"That arrogant, jumped-up *fraud* thought he could waltz in and steal my legacy..." Victor ranted bitterly. "After all my hard work researching and perfecting that recipe year after year before my attempt, Marco thought he could snap his fingers and break my record on the first try. *Hah*! Serves him right, the blustering fool..."

Claire's eyes widened. She paused the recording, mind racing. This went far beyond a simple feud over a decades-old record—the venom in Victor's voice hinted at a deep resentment.

She nearly jumped out of her skin as Leslie appeared at her shoulder.

"Oh, Leslie! I didn't see you there."

"Have you seen my father?" Leslie asked, scanning the pub. "I followed the blood here, and unless someone else burst a pint glass..."

Claire hesitated, glancing at the bathroom Victor hadn't emerged from yet. Given Victor's agitated state, she doubted Leslie's presence would improve matters.

"Already left, I'm afraid," Claire lied. She noticed Leslie blinking back tears and softened. "You look like you could use a chat?"

Leslie shrugged, but dropped into the armchair by the fireplace. She perched stiffly on the edge of the cushion.

"I'm sure your father was just... *surprised* by the announcement," Claire offered gently. "It's a big thing to take on."

Leslie's lip quivered. "He's never thought I could amount to *anything*. Never been proud of me, no matter how hard I try. I was so foolish to think this stunt could finally impress him. Prove I was good enough by taking on his legacy." She took a shaky breath, squaring her shoulders. "I don't need his approval anymore. This is *my* new beginning. Maybe I'll open my *own* restaurant, or go back to college to sharpen up my skills." She shuffled to the edge. "I should get back. Lots of planning to do."

"Before you go..." Claire scrambled, so many questions swirling in her mind. "I heard your father was involved in helping Marco prepare his attempt?"

Leslie paused, frowning into the flames. "Oh, that. When Marco first announced he was taking on the record, he visited my father for guidance. Tristan arranged it all. My father seemed pleased by the attention at first. He dug out all his old notes and recipes to share."

"But something changed?" Claire pressed.

Leslie's eyes narrowed. "Marco grew frustrated with Dad's fussing and trying to control everything. They clashed over ingredients and methods. Marco wanted to twist things, and I don't think he wanted my father's help. I think he wanted to get his blessing for the publicity. A coronation, of sorts, and Dad hated that. He's been clinging to that record ever since. It's like his whole life revolved around *that*." She sighed, shaking her head. "Even after all that record brought him, Dad could never get over the fact he didn't reach that tonne. Throughout my entire life, I've been in the shadow of that *stupid* pudding."

"I'm sorry, Leslie, that sounds—"

Victor burst from the bathroom, toilet paper wrapped around his hand like a mitten. Leslie's gaze snapped to Claire with a scowl.

"You said he'd left!" she cried, and any pretence of congeniality vanished.

Leslie charged after her father, but he stormed towards the exit without acknowledging her, the pub door slamming behind him with a bang that silenced all conversation.

Claire watched through the window as the daughter chased the father across the market. A knot formed in her stomach, confusion and questions swirling in her mind. She felt like she was drowning in an ocean of thick brandy sauce, grasping for answers that remained frustratingly out of reach.

But there were still other leads. Claire turned to the bar, where Theresa was alone, busying herself with lining up glasses with shaky hands. She thought back to what Granny Greta had overheard. Planting something to get Marco in trouble? Drastic measures? Her instincts bristled, sensing it was time to confront the pub owner. As Claire approached, Theresa nearly toppled the row of pint glasses.

"Sorry, I... I didn't mean to startle you," Claire said gently. "I just... I need to talk to you again."

Theresa paled, her eyes growing round with apprehension. "W-what is it?"

Claire recounted what Granny Greta had overheard about planting evidence against Marco. "Theresa, please, if you know anything or were planning something..."

Theresa's composure shattered. Tears springing forth, she dropped her head into her hands against the bar. Between heaving sobs, the story spilt out.

"It's all true. We were *desperate*," she confessed. "Marco's flashy new menu could have destroyed everything we've built. There's not much money in what we do here to start with. We barely break even some weeks, but we stay here and keep pulling because we love it. Being here with our regulars... this place is our *home*. We had to do *something* before we lost it all to the *other* pub." She lifted her head, eyes pleading. "You must understand, Claire. I never meant for it to go so far, but Malcolm thought if we planted something to get Marco in trouble, it might save us..."

"So, you intended to frame Marco?" Claire asked gently. "Did you...?"

"No! *Never*." Theresa gripped Claire's hands with

ferocity. "We'd never actually hurt anyone. We just wanted Marco out of the way until business recovered. We made empty threats, but murder?" Her lip trembled. "I swear we had no part in what happened to that poor man. And we never got to planting anything. We chickened out. We'd had one too many pints of our own homebrew when we cooked up that plan. I swear, Claire… it was *all* talk…"

Claire studied Theresa's tear-stained face, seeing the toll recent events had taken. She believed the woman's claims of innocence, and Claire pulled Theresa into a comforting embrace. But Theresa's version of events was only one half of the Richards' story. Malcolm's alibi had still yet to be proved, and Claire couldn't shake the image of Malcolm rushing back in all dishevelled directly after Marco's stabbing.

CLAIRE EXITED THE PARK INN FEELING DEFLATED, THE weight of her accusation pressing on her shoulders. Lost in thought, she nearly collided with a familiar figure browsing the market stalls—Detective Inspector Ramsbottom.

"Oh, hello there, Claire!" Ramsbottom greeted, gloved hands clutching several hefty shopping bags. "Just picking up a few Christmas things for Mrs Ramsbottom.

Never too early to get a jump start on next Christmas, I always say."

Claire managed a weak smile, envying his untroubled cheer. "That's very proactive of you. How's the investigation coming along?"

"Slowly but surely, slowly but surely," Ramsbottom replied, sucking the chilly air through his teeth. He clapped a hearty hand on Claire's shoulder. "You're looking a bit peaky, my dear. Fancy joining me for a spot of mulled wine? My treat."

Before she could protest, he steered her towards the mulled wine stand, fishing coins out of his pocket with a whistle. Claire accepted the steaming paper cup, the rich, spiced aroma warming her chilled nose and lifting her spirits.

"So," Ramsbottom began, smacking his lips after a long sip, "any new insights into our line-up of suspects after your interviews?"

Claire hesitated, still feeling raw and uncertain after Grant waved a knife at her. "I'm still not entirely convinced about Malcolm and Theresa. They seemed genuinely shocked when I questioned them, but Malcolm's alibi is Drunken Pete, and I haven't seen him to check."

Ramsbottom nodded along. "Well, I should be getting the autopsy report soon, and then we'll be able to pinpoint a more precise time frame to verify everyone's alibis once and for all." He leaned in closer, dropping his voice conspiratorially. "But I still think that Elena woman is the most likely culprit in my book. Breaking things off with Marco the very night before his big event? Mighty suspicious timing, wouldn't you say?"

Claire shook her head. "I'm starting to realise there's more nuance to that love triangle than we first thought. It turns out Elena dated Grant before Marco arrived on the scene. So if this murder does stem from romantic motives, I'd be more inclined to suspect Grant than her at this point. Grant ended things with Elena, but I'd say Grant still resented Marco for picking up where he left off."

"Is that so?" Ramsbottom straightened with interest, his eyes brightening. "Well now, perhaps I ought to have another little chat with this Grant fellow. He's certainly got a temper on him." He tipped back the remainder of his mulled wine with relish. "Thank you for the nibble of insider information, Claire. Your unique insights on our suspects are always much appreciated." With a wink, he bustled off towards the pub, bags swinging.

Alone once more, Claire wandered back towards her shop, her thoughts as turbulent as the snow flurries gusting through the market. She pulled Ryan's mobile from her pocket and clicked play on his recorded interview with Victor earlier that afternoon, pressing the phone close to her ear. She listened intently to Victor's aggrieved ranting as she wound through the stalls, hoping his bitter words could clarify amidst the chaos. But the further she walked, the fainter Victor's resentful voice became, drowned out by the howling winds and the clamour of her self-doubt.

By the time Claire reached her candle shop, she had finished both the wine and the recording, yet felt no closer to unravelling the messy knot of lies and motives surrounding Marco's murder. With a resigned sigh, she pushed open the door and slipped back inside her little haven, yearning for the simplicity of dripping wax and wafting aromas. At least here among the rows of jars, her purpose was clear.

If only the messy matters of what drove people to kill could be solved as quickly as selecting the perfect formulas for her scented candles.

CHAPTER TWELVE

*C*urled on the sofa between Ryan and a sleepy Amelia, the opening scenes of *Shrek 2* played on the TV in her tiny flat above her shop. Hugo sprawled on his stomach on the floor, colouring in the accurate *Super Mario* Ryan drew for him. Claire reached out and plucked a handful of chocolates from the Celebrations box amidst the drying New Year's cards scattered across the coffee table. She dropped a chocolate into Ryan and Amelia's outstretched palms and tossed one to Hugo.

Her concerns about the investigation had faded into the background. With her family surrounding her, she relaxed into the cosy normality. An arts and crafts night with Ryan and the kids had been just what Claire had needed.

"Have you caught the bad guy yet, Claire?" Amelia asked as a yawn unfurled.

"Not yet, little one."

"Why don't you go to bed?" Ryan reached around and ruffled Amealia's hair. "It's been a long few days."

"Not tired," she said, yawning again as she leaned closer to *Shrek*. "Don't use all the ink in my new felt tips, Hugo."

"I'm not."

"That red one looks almost finished."

"But Mario *is* red."

"So, make him pink? I'm never going to use those."

While the children bickered back and forth and Ryan turned up the TV to drown them out, Claire's mind strayed back to the recording on the phone. Glancing at the engrossed faces of Ryan and the kids at the ogres quietened things down; she slipped an earbud into her ear and hit play on Ryan's phone to listen to Victor's diatribe again.

Victor's hostile tones filled her ear. "Do you know the *effort* it took to make a record-breaking thousand-pound plum pudding? I spent eighteen-hour days for *months* testing and perfecting the recipes. I drove across the county weekly to find the rarest, *best* ingredients money could buy. I *refused* to settle for anything less than absolute *perfection*."

Claire understood his dedication. She'd wanted the

same for her vanilla bean formula back at the factory. But even after it was stolen, she didn't think she ever spoke about it with as much bitterness as Victor, and she hadn't tried to make the largest candle in Northash to prove how great it was.

"But it was worth it," Ryan said in the recording, the tap running in the background; she imagined him cleaning Victor's wounded palm. "You set the record, and nobody has broken it since."

Victor continued, "And what did it get me? My restaurant struggled under mountains of debt. That pudding brought me my wife, Wendy, but I couldn't let it go. Two pounds shy of a tonne. All that time and money… I *couldn't* let it go. I kept trying, and I fell apart from the strain. I ended up losing everything—my restaurant closed, Wendy divorced me and then died, and my daughter disappointed me, never living up to my name. *My* legacy from that record is all *I* have left."

"I'm sure that's not true," Ryan assured him. "You still have your daughter. She came from your marriage, and your marriage came from that record."

"And that Marco thought he could just waltz in and outshine *my* greatest achievement?" Victor continued, his resentment thickening. "After I lost my restaurant, my wife, my pride… I'd have been damned if I'd let him steal my crown after *one* attempt!"

A loud advert jingle for car insurance interrupted

Claire's focus. She glanced up to see Hugo still immersed in his colouring, and Amelia had fallen asleep with her head on Claire's shoulder. Beside her, Ryan was the only one watching the film, chuckling to himself as Donkey was transformed into a white stallion after drinking Fairy Godmother's 'Happy Ever After' potion. She squeezed his hand, wishing they could discuss the revelations swirling in her mind. But with the kids present, she tucked the earbud back into her palm and cuddled up to him.

By the time the credits for *Shrek 2* rolled, both kids had drifted to sleep. Claire gathered up their arts and crafts mess while Ryan carried their sleeping forms to their beds in the guest room.

Alone at last, Claire sank onto the sofa beside Ryan, fresh mugs of hot chocolate and a plate of ginger nuts on the coffee table before them. Beyond the frosted window, all was still in the slumbering village square. She curled against him with a tired sigh, the stress of recent days nagging at her eyelids.

"I listened to some of Victor's recording again while you were watching the film," she began. "He seems to resent Marco. Like that record was the only thing left, giving his life meaning after everything else fell apart. Almost sounded like a confession."

"That's what I thought too, but I thought I might be reading too far into it." Ryan's arm tightened around her.

"Can't have been easy watching Marco get attention for attempting the very thing that ruined Victor's life, but… it's just a plum pudding."

"The resentment spreads to his daughter, too," Claire mused. "It's like the final insult in his final years."

"I can't imagine a world where I wouldn't support Amelia. I paint, she likes art… my mum painted too, and she encouraged me. I'd never discourage Amelia from trying to outdo me. In fact, that's what parents *should* want for their kids, but to hear Victor call Leslie a disappointment? That stung *me*, so how must that make her feel to know that's what he father thinks of her?"

Claire's heart twinged. She thought of her father, Alan, in his potting shed, always so supportive her and her dreams. Even her more critical mother had never stood in her way. After a silence, she shifted to meet Ryan's green eyes, still lingering on the sleeping village.

"I haven't told you everything that happened today," she confessed, glancing at the closed guest bedroom door. "When I confronted Grant earlier, I pushed too far, too recklessly…" Her voice hitched. She gripped his hand, finding courage in its strength. "He threatened me, Ryan."

"*Threatened*?" Ryan's solid muscles tensed as he bolted upright. "What did he say?"

"It's not so much what he said. It's what he did. He grabbed a knife."

"A *knife?*" Ryan sprung to his feet. "That's it, I'm going—"

"He only waved it at me, but..." Sighing, she wondered if she should have said anything. "In that moment, I thought he might stab me right there."

"I'm—"

"Barging in there will only make things worse," she said, pulling him back to the sofa. "As flattered as I am that you'd want to jump to my defence, if Grant did kill Marco, there's no saying he wouldn't stab you, too. I'm fine," she insisted. "I got out of there, and then Leslie delivered her toast, and things took a different turn."

"Were you alone with him?"

She nodded.

"Claire, you can't keep putting yourself in harm's way. This investigation... it's too dangerous." His voice softened. "I know you're invested, but Marco—he isn't worth you risking everything for. Your safety, your life..."

Claire blinked back sudden tears as she held his earnest gaze. His words echoed the swelling doubts and fears she'd been trying to suppress since that moment in the kitchen. With so many unanswered questions surrounding the suspects—and a killer still at large—she knew it would be wiser to walk away, to let Ramsbottom try to handle the rest.

And yet...

Her eyes drifted to the darkness beyond the window

where the giant plum pudding tent stood—Marco's unfinished legacy, a symbol of his ambition and the turmoil left in his wake.

Somewhere in that tangle of lies and festering resentment, the truth waited.

She thought of her father again, and the career he'd dedicated to seeking justice for others, no matter how messy or difficult the path. In her bones, she knew walking away now would betray everything her instincts told her. If Leslie had giant plum pudding records in her blood, Claire had sleuthing in hers.

"You *know* I can't stop. Not yet. I'm too close, too involved now. This mystery has its hooks in me, dangerous or not." She squeezed his hand, willing him to understand. "Tomorrow, I'm going back to the beginning. I'll re-interview everyone, and... I don't know. Find the answers. Whatever it takes to unravel this knot. Will you still help me?"

Ryan studied her for a long moment, his eyes clouded. But slowly, he nodded, a wry smile touching his lips.

"Partners to the end," he affirmed.

"Partners to the end," she agreed, resting her head on his chest. "And let's hope someone slips up tomorrow. Four days till New Year's Eve, and I'd like to welcome next year without this shadow looming over Northash."

CHAPTER THIRTEEN

*C*laire hurried across the quiet village square, her breath fogging the icy air. She was determined to confront each suspect to gauge their reactions. She had to uncover if any were hiding crucial information that could help solve Marco's murder.

Her first stop was the kitchen at The Park Inn. Claire entered through the rear delivery door, hoping to catch Grant unawares. She found him alone, furiously chopping vegetables on the stainless-steel countertop, movements rigid and jerky. At the sight of her slight frame lingering in the doorway, he slammed the knife down with a loud clatter, and this time, Claire kept her distance.

"What the hell are you doing back here *again*?" he

snapped, eyes flashing. "Didn't I make myself clear yesterday?"

Claire raised both palms, striving for a non-threatening tone. "I apologise for the intrusion, Grant. I know you're busy preparing for the dinner shift." She took a cautious step forward. "But I can't help but feel there are still pieces missing."

Grant's glare remained suspicious and unwavering. "Yeah, well, I already told the police everything I know. Why don't you and the rest of this bloody village leave me in peace?"

Sensing Grant's volatility simmering below the surface, Claire changed tacks, hoping an appeal to his ego might make him lower his guard. "As the new head chef, I imagine all this attention on the investigation is disruptive for you. I was hoping for *your* insider's perspective on things. That's all I want."

For a moment, Grant looked thoughtful, but then his expression shuttered again. "Yesterday, you were accusing me of murder. I'm not simple, Claire. I want nothing more to do with any of it. It's over and done with, as far as I'm concerned." He roughly swept the chopped vegetables into a waiting pan. "Now, are you ordering something or not? 'Cause otherwise, get out of my kitchen before I call the police on you for trespassing, and don't think I won't."

Claire backed towards the exit door, rebuffed by

Grant's refusal to engage, though he was right; she had accused him yesterday, and she'd gone to speak with him first expecting as much. Still, it seemed clear he was hiding something, but his firm stare told her nothing would be gained by pushing him further today. She would have to find alternate routes to the truth, and he *was* still clutching a knife.

Her next stop was Leslie's cupcake stall on the market, but Claire found only an abandoned wooden stand. The annoyed woman at the neighbouring jewellery kiosk told her Leslie had unexpectedly packed up her things early that morning, claiming a vague family emergency.

Unease pricked at Claire as she crossed the square lanes towards Ryan's gym where she'd first spoken with Tristan Raybourn on the treadmills. Inside the brightly lit fitness centre, Claire wove between clusters of rumbling exercise equipment, scanning for any glimpse of Tristan's imposing frame.

Instead, she spotted her boyfriend Ryan at the front desk, logging entries on the computer. When she approached, he broke into a welcoming smile.

"Ready for another round already?"

Claire shook her head. "Not today, I think I pulled something last time. I was hoping to have a word with Tristan. Any sight of him?"

"Haven't seen him since he was last in here when you spoke to him. Missed his regular times, and that's not like him." Ryan's expression shifted to one of understanding. He rifled through a drawer and pulled out an ornate business card. "He left this behind a while ago. It has his office details if you want to try reaching him there."

Claire thanked him, tucking the thick cardstock into her pocket. She knew phoning Tristan's secretary was a long shot, but she'd run out of options.

"Worth a shot," she said. "Dinner at the cul-de-sac tonight?"

"I'd love that. My shift ends in an hour, so I can swing by your shop to pick you up when you're closing. Maybe you'll have sorted this whole mess by then."

"I hope so. I think Dad's only invited me to pick me brains about the case."

Leaving Ryan to get back to work, Claire found a sheltered alcove outside the gym and dialled the number engraved on Tristan's flashy business card. After three rings, a clipped female voice answered.

"Tristan Raybourn Enterprises, how may I help?"

Claire took a bracing breath. "Hello, my name is Claire Harris, and I am calling for Mr Raybourn. I have some urgent questions regarding the recent troubling events regarding one of his employees, Marco? Could you please put me through to him?"

"I deeply apologise, but Mr Raybourn is currently busy conducting an important business meeting," the brisk secretary replied after a pause. "He left strict instructions *not* to be disturbed. I'd be happy to take a message?"

Frustrated but unsurprised, Claire asked for when she could expect a return call but only received a vague assurance that Mr Raybourn's would be 'indefinitely' busy. As the line disconnected, Claire shivered in the icy alcove, picturing Tristan hiding in his office, refusing her call. She imagined his hand hesitating over the button, suspicion in his eyes that she was unravelling too many threads. The thought chilled her more than the winter wind.

Back out in the knife-edged wind, Claire approached the lane where Elena's clothing boutique was tucked away. She prayed the soft-spoken woman with the mournful eyes hadn't also inexplicably vanished like Leslie.

Breathless, Claire pushed inside Still Loved, smiling despite her worry when she recognised the cashier behind the counter. Claire knew Lena from a previous visit, easily recognisable from her elaborate orange headscarf holding back long ginger dreadlocks framing her brown freckled face.

"Claire, hello again! Here to treat yourself to some new threads?" Lena's bright tone faltered when she noted Claire's taut expression. "Everything alright, love?"

Claire took a bracing breath. "I was hoping to have a

quick word with Elena if she's working today? It's rather important."

At the mention of her name, Lena's kohl-rimmed eyes immediately dimmed. She fiddled with an eyebrow piercing between perfectly manicured fingernails. "I'm so sorry to tell you this, but Elena quit yesterday without notice."

Claire's heart sank. She had feared as much. "Do you know where she was heading when she left?"

Lena shook her head, dreadlocks swinging. "Afraid not. None of us have been able to reach her. It was all very sudden and strange." She looked beyond Claire, gaze distant. "I didn't even get a chance to say a proper goodbye. She'd become one of my closest friends here, always willing to listen, but she just said she'd had enough and wouldn't be coming back. We were meant to get curry and go dancing next weekend. She'd finally agreed to let me give her a makeover." A wistful half-smile ghosted her lips. "Said she wanted to reinvent herself, become someone new..."

"I'm sorry, Lena."

"Elena has been so on edge since Marco died. She told me she needed to get away from Northash immediately, make a clean break." Sighing, she leaned closer and added, "He was never the right fit for her. Too far up his own backside, but Elena always saw the best in people. Do you think she's in some kind of trouble?"

Claire managed what she hoped was a reassuring smile despite the unease spiking within her. "I'm sure Elena is fine. She probably needs time and space to heal after everything. But thank you for your help, Lena."

Claire's unease deepened as she exited the empty shop. First Leslie, now Elena. Was someone deliberately ensuring the suspects became unavailable just as she redoubled her investigation efforts?

She set off back towards her shop, though the entrance of Starfall Park further up the steep lane caught her eye. A familiar head of thick grey hair poked out from under a hat as Victor limped through the gates.

"*Victor*!" Claire called out, quickening her pace. "Victor, wait!"

The old man didn't slow, shoulders hunched inside a voluminous coat as he disappeared down the winding path into the park's Chinese garden. Claire hustled after him, nearly losing her footing on the snow-slicked pavement.

"Victor?" she panted, as he retreated. "I just want to talk and see how your hand is doing."

If he heard her appeals over the whistling wind, Victor gave no indication. Claire scrambled to keep up as he wound through the tranquil landscape of arched bridges, gazing pools and mossy sculptures now covered in a frosted white sheen. Unease skittered through Claire. She took a hesitant step back, a dry twig snapping under her boot. Victor's hooded head jerked up, glassy eyes fixing unerringly on her, half-obscured behind a tree.

Claire fully expected irate vitriol or even another violent outburst. But Victor merely stared at her for a taut moment before turning wordlessly back to his task. He pulled a bottle of what looked like rum from a plastic bag and made himself comfortable on a bench, sitting in the middle and taking up the space. She considered approaching, but he gulped down a good amount of the rum, and it didn't look like his first drink of the day, either.

Deciding against walking head first into an interview with a drunk in a quiet corner of the park, Claire retreated the way she'd come. So much for spending her afternoon reinterviewing the suspects...

CHAPTER FOURTEEN

t her parents' cul-de-sac, Claire surveyed the darkened windows of the vacant where Mrs Beaton used to live. The 'For Sale' sign had been jutting from the overgrown lawn since the previous autumn, with no interest in the old rundown house. She sighed, picturing the bygone days of her childhood when their whacky neighbour had lived there with her army of cats.

"They've just dropped the price again," Ryan said, looping his fingers through hers. "Sally keeps sending me links. Almost identical in layout to the house next to your parents'." He looked off to the house he grew up in. "Oh, the 'For Sale' sign has gone. Someone must have bought it."

"Then my parents are getting new neighbours in the new year, I suppose." But Claire's attention was still on

Mrs Beaton's old place. "This is a little fixer-upper, but can't you see it when it's done? It would look like every other house in the cul-de-sac. Better, even."

Ryan smiled, though it didn't quite meet his eyes. "We'd make quite the DIY team, wouldn't we? But first things first... a mortgage deposit. We're still nowhere near. We'd never get accepted."

"Sally said we wouldn't know unless we went through the motions of an application."

"Next year?" he suggested. "You never know. We might win the lottery before then."

"Do you even play the lottery?"

"No. But I could start?"

They laughed, and Claire returned to studying the peeling paint and overgrown garden. They'd only talked about the idea of getting somewhere together for them and the kids earlier that year, but getting that mortgage with Ryan seemed a distant priority amidst the chaos and mysteries swirling around her. With a last lingering look, she turned towards her parents' home, golden light spilling from the windows in welcome.

"If you started selling your paintings…"

"Claire…"

"They *are* good enough, Ryan," she assured him. "And come the new year, when I win that bet, and you get accepted into a gallery, you'll see it too." Smiling up at him, she said, "Half of your cards have flown off the shelves with a little nudge from the sale, though my mother's choice of wording for my banner has every other customer asking if we're closing down."

"Don't even think about it."

"I think Claire's Candles has much more left in the tank, right?" She winked, letting go of his hand to open her childhood front door, staring off to the silhouette of the dark candle factory on the hill. "Damon was even talking about a second shop… could you imagine? From factory to franchise in only a few short years."

"Yes, I can," he said, kissing her on the cheek from behind. "Because it's you, and you're brilliant. You're more brilliant than you'll give yourself credit for. Now, let's get inside before we freeze to death. All people have been discussing in the gym all day is that we're about to be buried under two feet of snow by the morning."

Inside the house, always toasty from the always burning radiators, she found her mother in the sitting room, wielding her portable carpet cleaner, aggressively scrubbing and sucking Greta's Baileys stain from the armchair arm. Before she was roped into helping, Claire dragged Ryan down the hallway and into the kitchen.

"I'll keep guard here," Ryan said, helping himself to the kettle. "I'll have a coffee waiting for your return."

"You spoil me."

"Only because you deserve it."

After a quick kiss, Claire hopped down the stepping

stones to the bottom of the garden and ducked into the potting shed. Her father glanced up from the seed trays lined before him, features softened by the glow of the heat lamp overhead. He set down his trowel, brushing potting soil from his worn gardening gloves.

"Come in from the cold, little one," Alan welcomed, beckoning her. "The daffodil bulbs will have to wait for my super sleuth daughter. How are you getting on with the case?"

Claire sighed, perching on her plant pot. "I wish I could say I had it in the bag. Tried to talk to all the suspects again today."

"Tried?"

"And failed." She held her hands out to the small gas heater. "They all dodged me."

"Ah." He nodded, considering his response. "I can see your dilemma. No access to your suspects means... no case. Not until there's a new development, at least."

"I feel like I keep uncovering new questions instead of answers," she said, rubbing her palms. "But it must be one of them, mustn't it? Marco didn't reach around and stab himself."

"The path to truth seldom runs smooth or straight in this line of work," he offered. "But your persistence and courage will uncover it, little one. Now tell me, what revelations have you gathered since we last spoke?"

As Claire recounted her latest findings regarding

Grant's kitchen outburst, Leslie's announcement, and Victor's bad attitude, her doubts and worries tumbled in a flood. The risks she'd taken, the dangers she'd recklessly rushed into, the assumptions that had led her to her current dead end. Still, her father listened, nodding and taking time to chew over the details.

"Maybe I'm in over my head?" he said finally.

Alan leaned forward, holding her gaze and then her hands. She didn't mind that he had on his muddy gardening gloves.

"Claire, they said I was a fine detective back in my day, and I know you possess the same instincts that gave me my career before my damn foot forced me into retirement." He paused to whack his bad leg. "If I learned anything, solving a complex case requires more than clues. It takes understanding the human element—the motivations, secrets, and messy emotions that drive people to kill. None of those people are likely to confess. The question you should be asking is..."

"Who wanted Marco dead the most?"

"*Exactly*, little one." His face lit up, and he let go of his hands. Spinning back to his potting desk, he tugged off his gloves and rummaged around in a drawer for a pen, a pad, and a ball of brown string. "Go over those suspects again, and we'll make a board. I never felt like I was investigating a case without a wall to stare at. You'd be surprised what you can uncover with drawing pins and string."

Comforted by his wisdom, Claire watched as her father scribbled down all her thoughts. When he finished, he returned to the house to grab them cups of coffee, leaving her to assemble the board on the shed wall with the pins and strings.

Claire sighed as she stuck Marco's name in the middle, disliking him the more she learned. The vision of the charismatic head chef had been replaced by an evil man who'd piggybacked off those around him for fifteen minutes of fame.

Next, she added his ex-girlfriend, Elena's, name. Though she'd discovered the body, Elena seemed the least likely killer. She had wanted to go to the police about something, and Claire needed to find out what.

Next was Leslie. Her moods fluctuated wildly, and she'd gained—or regained—from Marco's death in the form of a job at the pub. But was that enough motive?

Grant had gained the most—the promotion he craved. Without Marco, he could finally cook freely. But his temper concerned Claire, especially after his threat, which had only come when she'd suggested his guilt. He also had the most written about him. She connected a string from Grant to Elena.

Tristan remained an enigma. He was ruthless and had wanted Marco to repay his loan, but murder seemed extreme. As a businessman, Tristan surely wouldn't kill over £20,000, especially now it meant there was no way he'd get his money back. But again, she didn't know if he could be trusted.

And then there was Victor. He was obsessed to the end with his plum pudding record, unable to move on. His single-minded pursuit of glory had cost him everything. Could that drive him to kill the man who took it all away?

Claire stepped back and studied the board. She knew what questions to ask, but getting them alone would be hard. Confronting them together could backfire but might reveal more, but how?

She picked up a pen to start writing her questions down when the shed door burst open. She spun around, expecting to see her father, but it was Ryan.

"DI Ramsbottom's stress-eating a trifle," he said. "You'll want to come and hear this."

Claire pulled the shed door shut and followed Ryan back to the house. Her mother and father stood over DI Ramsbottom as he dug through layers of cream, cake and fruit with a giant silver serving spoon.

"That was supposed to be for New Year's Eve," Janet muttered. "Slow down, Harry, or you'll choke to death!"

"What is it, Harry?" Alan asked, his voice much softer. "Save some for the rest of us, old friend."

"So sorry," he muttered, turning the spoon to Alan. He

shook his head at the offer and gobbled another mouthful. "There have been some developments…"

"Developments?" Claire ventured, never having seen him so stressed.

"Good news or bad news?" he asked, dropping the splash into the bowl with a splash. Janet sighed as cream dotted the island, and she swooped in with a cloth. "Good news first, eh? According to the autopsy report, Marco's official time of death was between 6:20 and 6:30 p.m. on Christmas Eve, which gives us a solid window to confirm alibis to start ruling people out."

"That's not good news," Alan said, "that's *great* news. A proper breakthrough, at last."

Ramsbottom nodded his agreement, his eyes following the trifle as Janet whisked it away. She replaced it with a glass of water and he gulped half down in seconds.

"And the bad news?" Claire asked, almost not wanting to know.

After a pause to dab his lips with the end of his tie, Ramsbottom exhaled and said, "There's been another attack."

"Oh, dear," Janet cried. "Another stabbing? What is this place coming to?"

"Not a stabbing. A *bricking*." Ramsbottom let his tie flap down as he mimed a solid whack. "Behind The Park Inn. It's Leslie… she's…. she's *dead*."

CHAPTER FIFTEEN

tunned just beyond the police tape behind The Park Inn, Claire stared at the spot where Leslie lay crumpled just an hour before as the police officers hurried to erect a tent over the scene. The thick flakes of fluffy snow worked to obscure the dark stain seeping across the icy cobbles.

She couldn't comprehend it.

Leslie had been murdered.

Just like Marco.

She wiped the tears tumbling down her cheeks with her coat sleeve as the bitter wind whipped through the alley behind The Park Inn. The black spot of the pudding tent had leaked out, its shadow stretching further across Northash; the strange week between Christmas and New Year had never felt more like limbo.

Detective Inspector Ramsbottom approached, his expression grim as he scratched at his golden hair.

"Terrible, terrible business," he said, shaking his head. "I wish there were more I could have done to stop this happening, but how could we predict something like this? A brick to the head... so *senseless*."

Just then, Claire noticed the offending brick. A plain red brick—Nori, from the stamp—old, unremarkable, dense, and as solid as iron. The attacker had left it on the cobbles, blood still peppering the edge. She imagined them striking, noticing what they'd done, then dropping it before they fled, leaving Leslie to succumb to her fate.

Left out in the cold.

"The stabbing with the missing knife in the kitchen tent felt premeditated," she said, scanning the area for similar bricks. She nodded at the wall separating the alley behind the pub from the park where the pointing had eroded, and several bricks were missing. "Spur of the moment, this time. Could it have been the result of an argument?"

"Given the blood, we believe Leslie was struck from behind while fleeing her attacker and staggered a few feet before collapsing," Ramsbottom said, sounding as queasy as Claire felt. "I'd say your assumption is a correct one. Whoever Leslie was out here with, perhaps they didn't intend to kill her. Not at first, at least, but you're right... snap decisions can change everything."

Claire pictured the altercation in her mind, Leslie glancing back in terror as she ran, never seeing the fatal blow coming. She clasped her gloved hands together, willing them to stop shaking.

"I spoke with her yesterday afternoon," Claire said, her voice barely louder than a whisper. "Even with everything going on, she seemed more herself. Excited about the future. And I still suspected her…"

"At least we can rule her out now." Ramsbottom sighed. "No, not much of a consolation, I know. My team is searching the surrounding area for any sign the killer is still lurking, but I can't see anyone hanging around in this snow." He paused, glancing around before lowering his voice. "My sergeant noticed something curious under her fingernails. Small bits of skin, likely from scratching her attacker. And the skin was purplish, like she'd scratched off an existing bruise."

"A bruise?" Claire echoed. "Maybe from an altercation with Marco?"

"Something to investigate. A scratch that deep can't be hidden."

As Claire tried to mentally assess if she'd noticed bruises on any of the suspects, a young officer beckoned Ramsbottom back to the scene. With an apologetic look, the detective ducked under the police tape, leaving Claire shivering on the edge of the crime scene.

She stared up at the looming backside of The Park

Inn, its twinkling string lights seeming garish and taunting now. Marco, their new head chef murdered a stone's throw away, and now their rehired sous-chef, Leslie, bricked down outside its back door. Two murders in one week, both connected to one pub. Fear crept its icy fingers around Claire's heart—would there be a third?

After staring at the murderous brick one last time, Claire left the alley and walked back to the front of the pub. She found Ryan, shoulders hunched against the wind, snowflakes clinging to his woolly hat, waiting for her by the front door. He was behind the barrier of a second cordon set up to keep the crowd at bay, watching the unfolding scene despite the snow falling heavier by the second.

She slipped into his arms, pressing her face against his coat.

"I think we should go home," Ryan suggested, his breath warm against her hair. "You're going to catch your death."

Claire shook her head, looking up at him with resolve. "Later. I want to find out more about what happened here. We're inside the cordon, after all."

The officer blocking the pub's front door stepped aside to let them in, and the pub's dining space seemed hollow and empty without the sea of customers. Plates piled with dinner and glasses topped with drinks stood abandoned on tables with chairs left at jaunty angles. A scene frozen in time. Claire could hear the scraping of chair legs on the floorboards as chaos swept through the pub after the discovery of Leslie's body.

Ramsbottom had come in from the cold, too, conferring with a uniformed officer in the kitchen doorway. He wrapped up the conversation when he noticed Claire and waved her over.

"You really shouldn't be here," he said, looking around as the forensic officers started to sweep through the place. "You should get yourself home. Get warmed up by the fire."

"I will," Claire said, looking past him and through to the back door open to the snow swirling around the alley. "Who found her?"

"One of the bartenders carrying an empty barrel up from the cellar," Ramsbottom said, rubbing his forehead. "Young lass. I doubt she'll sleep tonight. I've already interviewed the kitchen staff, and none claim to have heard anything, but the dining room was full."

Claire nodded, hearing an echo of the din of clattering cutlery competing with a chorus of conversation from her lunchtime visit the day before.

"According to the other staff, Leslie was here planning her pudding attempt with Tristan in *that* booth," he continued, pointing across the restaurant. "She left about twenty minutes before her estimated time of death. According to one of the kitchen staff, she went into the kitchen and was talking to Grant about ordering her new chef's whites. The conversation seemed amicable, and then she left through the back door around six."

"So, Grant and Tristan were both present, just like when Marco was stabbed," Ryan pointed out. "What about the others?"

"Elena *was* here too," Ramsbottom admitted in a whisper. "According to one of the bar staff, she was sat at the bar drinking wine. She asked several times when Grant was due to finish his shift. If the timeline from the statements is correct, she left through the front door sometime after Leslie."

"Easy enough to walk around the back," Claire said, having just done the same. "And Victor?"

"No sign of him, but like you said, anyone could have walked around the back. We're checking Leslie's phone records to see if she called anyone there to meet her." He scanned the quiet restaurant with a desperate sigh. "If he has any sense, he'll turn himself in for questioning, but at this very moment, my officers haven't been able to find him at his home."

"But he wouldn't kill his daughter, would he?" Ryan said.

"You'd hope not," Claire said, less sure.

"In my line of work, you stop thinking like that," Ramsbottom whispered with a knowing tap of his nose. "Nothing stranger than folk, lad."

"So, none of the suspects have an airtight alibi for Leslie's estimated time of death?" Claire said, letting the information churn over slowly. "And Vincent is missing."

"Seems that way."

"Earlier, at the cul-de-sac, you said something about a ten-minute window?" Ryan remembered. "For Marco's murder."

"Ah, yes." Ramsbottom patted down his jacket and flicked through. "According to the adjudicators, Marco left the tent for a cigarette break. They said he seemed stressed that the weighing was taking so long. He was out there for about fifteen minutes before Elena found him, but the autopsy report narrowed it down even further. Marco died somewhere between 6:20 and 6:30 p.m. Given what happened here tonight, I haven't had a chance to confirm any initial alibis for that time."

Claire nodded, thinking back to what she'd been doing before Leslie's murder sent everything spiralling sideways. She'd been in her father's shed going over the investigation board and had come up with an idea that felt less implausible now that she knew four of the suspects had been gathered in one place before one of them had a meeting with a brick.

"What if we got them all together?" Claire suggested. "The suspects. Confront them with what we know and see how they react and interact. Maybe we can catch one of them in a lie. See who'd want Marco *and* Leslie dead the most."

Ramsbottom considered this, rubbing his chin. "Hmm. It's not the worst idea I've heard. It's not like we have many leads. If I have my team here as backup..." He trailed off, thinking. "Yes, I quite like that. Claire, you could lead the questioning."

"*Me?*"

"You got Elena and Grant to open up more than I could. Or my officers, for that matter." Ramsbottom landed a heavy hand on her shoulder. "You have the same common folk touch that your father has. You're a Harris. I mean this with the greatest respect, but you're not intimidating." He deliberated, nodding to himself. "Yes, I'll try to round them up for an urgent meeting. Here, tomorrow morning. I'll be in touch." He slotted his pad away, patting down different pockets. "I never gave you this, okay?"

Ramsbottom folded a small black USB drive into her palm before rushing through the kitchen. Turning it over and wondering what could be on it, Claire left the pub with Ryan and ducked under the police tape, stepping out into the frigid air that enveloped Northash. As they walked towards her candle shop around the corner, the ordinarily short journey felt longer.

Ryan touched Claire's arm as she dug out her keys with clumsy gloved fingers. "Are you sure about this? Putting yourself in the hot seat like that?"

She paused on the threshold, looking back at the deserted square. The rest of the Christmas market had been disassembled, leaving only the white kitchen tent back. Presumably for Leslie's record attempt—even more ill-fated than Marco's.

Claire's eyes landed on a figure staggering towards the glow of The Hesketh Arms. Recognising Drunken Pete, Claire passed the shop keys to Ryan.

"Get the heating on? I need to confirm something."

She hurried across the icy cobbles and slipped into the pub's backyard. In the shadowy corner, she found Pete, face flushed and swaying.

"Well, hullo there!"

"Pete? I was hoping to find you." Claire hurried over. "Tell me, were you out here talking to Malcolm earlier this evening?"

"Why shure I wash!" Pete hiccupped, grinning sloppily. "Me 'n Malcolm, we talk mosht every night." His words ran together, almost indecipherable. "Don' remember bout what though..."

"But you and he were both here, around six o'clock or so?" Claire pressed.

"Time means nuthin' to old Pete." He blinked slowly. "But if ye say sho, mus' be true!"

"And what about the day of the plum pudding?" she pressed, unsure if there was any point. "When that chef was killed? Did you hear a woman screaming?"

"Woman scremin'?" He fished around inside his ragged coat, retrieving his battered mobile. "Rings a bell. Sho, Malcolm was out 'ere then, too. Lookit, I even took a pitcher. See?"

Peering at the dim screen, Claire made out Pete's blotchy face pressed against a disgruntled Malcolm. Time stamped across the bottom read 6:24 p.m. She exhaled with relief. Malcolm's alibi for Marco's was confirmed, and if Pete said Malcolm was there at six, she was glad to believe it.

"Thank you, Pete. This is hugely helpful." She checked her watch. "I should be getting back."

"Awroight then, luv. You have a merry Crispmas!" Pete lunged forward suddenly, planting a wet kiss on her forehead before breaking into song. "'*It was Christmas Eve babe, in the drunk tank...*'"

As Pete caterwauled *Fairytale of New York* at full volume, Claire slipped back around the pub and hurried across the deserted market square. Back at her dark candle shop, she found Ryan fiddling with the thermostat.

"Ramsbottom is right," she said, stomping the snow

off her boots. "For better or worse, people act differently when I ask them questions. Someone needs to do something."

Behind the counter, while the coffee machine crunched through a fresh batch of beans in the dark storeroom, Claire slotted the USB drive into the shop's laptop and pulled up a notepad while Ryan flicked through the few remaining cards on his display.

"What are you working on?"

"Questions for tomorrow. I want to be ready." Claire double-clicked on the drive, smiling. "Ramsbottom's given me a copy of the case files."

She clicked on the scan of Marco's recipe, including those Damson plums Victor had prized so much. She inhaled, the plum scent in the air turning her stomach. One-sniff wonders Claire would be happy to sell the final candle of.

"It's been a long day," Ryan said, pushing the laptop shut slightly. "Em's babysitting the kids back at my place tonight. You should get an early night. You'll want to be fresh for your big interview tomorrow."

"*If* Ramsbottom gets them all in the same room."

"I'm sure he will," Ryan said, opening the door to her flat. "Who wouldn't turn up? It'll only make them look guiltier."

Claire let Ryan tug her up from the counter up the narrow staircase to her flat. After they'd gone over

Claire's plan, Ryan fell asleep in minutes, but sleep eluded Claire as she lay curled beneath her duvet with Domino and Sid, listening to the wind howling outside. When it finally came, her dreams were troubled, full of dark alleyways and shadowy figures just out of sight, all in the shadow of a giant purple plum as big as Northash's square.

CHAPTER SIXTEEN

*C*laire leaned against the shop's counter, tapping her pen on her notepad to hone the questions for the imminent suspect interrogation.

Across from her, her father scrutinised the investigation board he'd transferred to a portable board —made from Christmas gift bags taped together— clutching his cane as he took in the web of photos, notes, and string.

"Building rapport is the *key* when you've got multiple suspects together in one room," he advised, pausing to tap on Marco's portrait pinned in the centre, adding pictures he'd cut out of the newspaper. "Make them feel at ease before confronting them with any damning evidence. If they all turn on you as a group, there's no hope of getting anywhere."

Claire nodded, jotting down his suggestion beneath her other scrawled notes. She hoped to confront Marco's murder suspects, as a group could elicit revealing reactions. Still, she also worried her plan could ultimately backfire if she didn't find the right balance of friendliness and confrontation. She'd already aggravated Grant and Tristan at different points, but at least she had Elena on her side; she couldn't imagine the sweetest of the suspects turning on her like the others.

The door rang out as DI Ramsbottom hobbled into the candle shop, his blonde toupee askew atop his head as the wind swirled outside—the piece usually defied the weather. Still, he'd been even more chaotic than usual since the start of this case.

"You'll *never* believe it!" he announced, a touch of manic excitement glinting his eyes. "Only gone and done it, haven't I? Managed to gather up all the suspects at The Park Inn—everyone *except* Victor. My officers are still looking, though. Victor must be somewhere."

Unless he's gone on the run, Claire thought, but she kept that to herself. She still couldn't fathom a father being able to murder his daughter, especially with the bluntness of a brick to the back of the brain. Still, she was impressed, as was her father, given his slow nod and outward curled bottom lip.

"How'd you manage it?" Alan asked. "Three out of four isn't bad."

"Your boyfriend, Ryan, gave me the idea," Ramsbottom said, nodding his thanks. "He was in Marley's first thing, and he said the suggestion that they'd look guiltier if they didn't attend would make up their minds. And it did! Had them all agreeing. Reluctantly so, but they're waiting there as we speak."

Claire's heart skipped several beats, half thrilled and half apprehensive now the moment she'd flippantly suggested yesterday was about to happen. She was eager to confront the suspects—the thought had kept her tossing and turning for most of the night—yet she felt unprepared, even with her long list of written questions.

"Are you tagging along, Dad?" she asked, hoping he'd say yes. "Could use your expert eye."

"You'll do splendidly without me holding your hand, little one," he assured. "I'll be of more use here giving Damon a hand with the shop."

On cue, Damon popped his scruffy head out of the storage room. "To be honest, Claire, I do much prefer working with your dad. He doesn't threaten to fire me when I read comics or play video games when it's quiet, and he whips me far less, too." He winked, passing her a hot cup of espresso. "Give them hell."

Claire tossed the coffee back in one bitter mouthful and, though reluctant to abandon Damon yet again during another of the sales days, opportunities like this one wouldn't wait around until closing. She put the cup on the counter, took a centring breath, and gave her father a determined nod before following Ramsbottom's shuffling footsteps into the snow-blanketed village square.

"Give them hell," her father called after her before the door shut.

"I'll try," she called. "And if you catch Damon engaging in nerd-based activities on the clock, the whip is in the drawer under the counter."

Ramsbottom chuckled as they set off around the corner, but he said, "You *are* joking, aren't you, Claire? It's *highly* illegal to whip your staff." He glanced at her arched brow and added, "Of course you're joking. Very funny. 'Banter'. Your father and I used to *banter* back in the good ol' days. He'd say, 'You're useless, Ramsbottom!' and I'd laugh." Pinching his brows, he thought about it momentarily before shaking his head. "Must say, it's nice to see him finally settling into his retirement years. His feet don't seem as itchy these days."

"Yeah, it is, isn't it?" Claire agreed with a smile, even if she wished he was accompanying her. "Is the pub busy?"

"Cleared it specially," he said with a wink. "Invoked crime scene privileges especially. Tristan wasn't happy he had to cancel the afternoon sittings." Leaning in as he pulled open the door, he whispered, "I had a little peek at the booking system, and it doesn't seem like these murders are scaring people away from the place. How times have changed for the *other* pub, eh?"

Stepping inside behind Ramsbottom, Claire was met with an eerie silence. The abandoned plates and glasses from the night before had been cleared, the chairs neat in rows upside down on the tables. Across the deserted dining room, beneath twinkling fairy lights, she could see Tristan, Grant, and Elena seated in the same booth where she'd had her Christmas lunch with Damon.

The same day Grant had waved a knife at her.

Tristan and Elena glanced in her direction, but Grant didn't look up from the beer mat he was spinning between his thumb and forefinger.

Taking in another deep breath, Claire moved to approach the suspects, quelling the sudden anxiety knotting in her stomach. She patted her pocket for her prepared questions, not that she'd put them in her pocket. She could see them clearly on the counter in the shop. Looking back at the door, she considered running around the corner for them, but there was no guarantee the three of them would be there when she returned. She tried to scan the list in her mind, but Grant's sudden eye contact spun through her. He offered a tight smile that she couldn't read. Here she was, about to interrogate three murder suspects with no solid plan. She'd have to wing it and hope for the best.

The pub door opened as she reached the booth. She

looked back, half-expecting her father to be waving the paper above his head, but she was surprised—and pleased —to see Ryan. He nodded his support before pulling down one of the chairs. Partners to the end. Suppressing a small smile at seeing him there, Claire gulped down her nerves and turned towards the suspects.

Tristan seemed irritated at being called in, arms crossed and jaw tense. Grant looked frustrated, spinning the beer mat faster with each rotation. Elena was the only one who offered Claire a genuine smile, though her eyes were downcast as she twisted a paper napkin around her fingers. Ramsbottom surprised Claire by diverting to the bar, leaving her alone at the booth.

With no time to consider her approach, she decided to open with the obvious.

"Thanks for coming, especially after what happened last night," she began, nodding towards the back of the pub—the bloodied brick flashed before her eyes, and she could imagine each of them holding it above their heads to strike Leslie down. "How are you all coping with the news?"

Elena exhaled. "I didn't know her well, but it's a heart-breaking tragedy. Such a pointless act."

Grant shrugged. "Can't say I liked her much—bad attitude and a rubbish cook, if you ask me. But no one deserves to get killed like that, do they? Hope she doesn't end up haunting the place." Elena shot him daggers across the table, and in a smaller voice, he said, "Kidding."

"Hilarious," Tristan said flatly as he checked his watch. "I'll have to begin the hassle of finding a new sous-chef; speaking of which, do you know how long this will take? I need to get the ad online if I want someone new by the end of the week."

"A woman died," Ryan called across the restaurant, his voice deeper and louder than Claire was used to hearing. "Have some respect."

"And may she rest in peace," Tristan replied with a mocking bow of his head. "But really, let's wrap this up quickly."

Claire gave them a moment, unsure of how to respond to the flippancy. She hadn't been Leslie's biggest fan, but she agreed with Ryan about the respect.

"I know this is a difficult time," she pushed, raising her voice, "so I will try to make this quick. Can you each account for your whereabouts last night after Leslie left the pub around six?"

Elena twisted her napkin. "I went straight home to my flat. Didn't want to miss the *Strictly* special."

"Ran out of potatoes, so I popped round to the grocer's for more," Grant offered casually. "Didn't hear about Leslie until I returned, and they wouldn't let me back in, so I went home."

Tristan sat back, steepling his fingers. "Urgent

conference call with some of my investment partners. They can verify the time stamps, I'm sure."

Claire glanced at Ramsbottom, who was opening a packet of pork scratchings he'd taken from behind the bar. She cleared her throat, and he snapped to attention, scooping up his pen to write the details in his pad. She glanced at Ryan, who could only offer a shrug.

"Let's go back to the night of Marco's murder," she began, deciding to go for directness despite her father's rapport advice; she wasn't going to get Grant and Tristan onside. "Specifically, the ten-minute window between twenty-past and half-past six on Christmas Eve."

Grant frowned. "I *already* told the police. After they wouldn't let me in the tent to talk to him, I returned to prepping the kitchen for the dinner service. Had to pick up his slack."

Tristan sniffed indignantly. "And as *I've* stated, I left the square about a quarter past to get to my scheduled training session with my fitness coach." He glanced at Ryan. "Different gym. Classier place. Private. You wouldn't know it, but he'll readily confirm my arrival."

"I was over at Still Loved, where I work. Was closing up before I f-found Marco," Elena added, her voice barely above a whisper as her eyes grew damp. "I think the cameras will have seen what time I left exactly, but I'm sure we didn't close until half-past. I just wanted to go and… and wish him luck…"

Grant let out an exaggerated huff. "Here come the waterworks." He rolled his eyes. "We've all got our stories straight, so can we wrap this up?"

Ignoring Grant's callousness, Claire decided to change direction and go for a more provocative line of questioning, since Grant had interacted with Elena.

"Grant... what exactly happened between you and Elena? You gave me the impression that Marco 'stole' her from you, but I heard through the grapevine that *you* ended things?"

Grant's eyes narrowed as he crossed his arms tighter across his chest. "I broke things off before the inevitable happened. Anyone could see she was making eyes at Marco from the moment he first showed up there. And a smug attention-seeker like Marco only wanted her because she was spoken for. So, I decided to save myself the hassle and got it over with."

"You *know* that's not how it was," Elena replied softly, still shredding the napkin. "I... I loved..."

"Sure *looked* that way when you shacked up with him straight away," Grant shot back. "I wasn't born yesterday."

Elena gazed down and repeated in a near-whisper, "It wasn't like that, though..."

"Mmhmm, keep telling yourself that."

"How... *domestic*." Tristan sighed, tugging his sleeve back to check his watch. "Somebody pull Jeremy Kyle out of retirement so we can wrap this up."

Sensing this line of inquiry could have been more productive. Claire decided to follow the flow to Elena. "I know you told me a little about your decision to end things with Marco, but why the night before his big record attempt?"

Elena kept her focus on the shredded napkin, avoiding Claire's gaze. "It wasn't intentional or planned... I couldn't pretend any longer. He was becoming more and more insufferable as the event grew closer. I guess the pressure got to him. Or maybe that's who he was. We only dated for a month or so, and he... wasn't the man I thought. I needed some peace away from the madness of—"

Just then, the pub's front door banged open. All heads turned to watch an unkempt Victor stumble inside, clutching a near-empty bottle of rum. An apprehensive policeman hovered behind him, a hand around his arm.

"What? None of you have ever gone out for a drink after a tragedy?" Victor slurred with an exaggerated sneer. He wavered slightly as the officer guided him over to the booth. "Get off me, pig."

"We found Mr Michaels sat on a park bench in Starfall Park by the pond," the officer explained to Ramsbottom. "Given the circumstances, we thought it best to bring him here."

"You can't drink that in here," Tristan called as Victor

dropped into the edge of the booth, stinking of booze. "You'll have to buy a drink from behind the bar."

"My daughter just died," he slurred, unscrewing the cap. It fell onto the floor, and he almost fell out of the booth to scoop it up. Claire darted down to pick it up. He held it out, and he snatched it with his palm, still wrapped in toilet roll, now stiff from patches of dried blood. "Anyone care to join me?" He offered the bottle around the table in a quick swoop before cramming it in his lips and muttering, "Too slow—"

Claire snatched the bottle from him and slammed it on the table behind her. Victor lunged for it, but the officer forced him back down.

"Party pooper," he grumbled. "Cheers for nothing."

The officer gave Ramsbottom a knowing nod before departing, clearly not keen on lingering. Victor made an unsteady attempt to slide back out of the booth.

"Right, well, I've shown my face, so now I'll be on my way."

Tristan instantly bristled, checking the gleaming watch on his wrist. "Well, if he's not staying, I'm not either."

But Ryan had already positioned himself in front of the exit, acting as an unofficial bouncer, his gym muscles never looking bigger as his thick arms folded against his even wider chest. "I think everyone's staying put until Claire gets some answers."

Ramsbottom's pork scratching gobbling sped up, but he didn't interject. Victor grumbled, sitting back down with the rest of them. Elena shuffled away a little, bumping into Tristan.

"Don't you all want the truth about what happened to your friend?" she asked, looking at Grant before looking at them each in turn. "Your business partners. Your ex-boyfriend. Your daughter." She paused on Victor, who, taken to staring into the middle distance, slumped to one side. "No one is leaving. Now, Tristan, let's go back to discussing that rather sizable loan you gave to Marco. Twenty thousand pounds, I believe? Help me understand how exactly you expected that to be repaid after it wasn't used for his plum pudding record attempt like he said it would be."

Tristan sighed, exasperated, as if the answer should be obvious. "Once I caught wind of what Marco blew it on instead, I knew that money was as good as gone. An expensive lesson learned." He gave an indifferent shrug. "Part and parcel of being in business—you win some, you lose plenty more."

Attention shifted to Victor as he shuffled off to raid the bar, only to have Ramsbottom swoop in and snatch away the pilfered full rum bottle before helping himself to another handful of pork scratchings. Shooting the detective an aggrieved scowl, Victor staggered back to collapse into the booth again.

"Right then, go on... ask me whatever intrusive questions you feel you must," Victor barked at Claire, words still slurred. "I've got nothing left to lose now, so don't hold back on my account."

Softening her tone, Claire asked, "I know discussing this must be difficult given your loss, but can you confirm where you were when Leslie was murdered yesterday? Around six?"

"Here and there."

"And when Marco was murdered? Between approximately twenty-past six and half-past on Christmas Eve?"

Victor waved his bandage, nearly losing his balance in the process. "There and here... wandering about through the crowded market, I suppose. I was quite distracted, so it's all a blur."

"How is your hand?" she asked. "You reacted strongly when you learned Leslie intended to try breaking your plum pudding record."

Victor let out a derisive snort. "That record was *mine*! The result of *years* of *my* blood, sweat, and tears. *I* was the one who did all the hard work researching and experimenting to make a thousand-kilogram pudding possible in the first place."

"Weren't you two pounds shy?" Grant muttered.

"Nobody would have even thought to attempt it if *I* hadn't done it first," Victor ranted. "*I* set the record."

Tristan couldn't suppress an exaggerated eye roll. "Oh, come off it, old man. It was a publicity stunt that was meaningless to anyone but you. Just let it go already. You got your glory days from it, didn't you?"

Victor slammed his bloodied fist down. "It meant *everything* to me. That record brought success to my restaurant. My wife accepted my proposal, and we had our beautiful daughter... it was *my* legacy!" He choked up, looking down to hide the glint of tears in his eyes.

Seizing on this reaction, Claire turned her focus to Tristan. "If achieving that record was so insignificant to *you*, why did you agree to provide funding for Leslie's attempt to break it?"

"Simple business decision," Tristan said, pausing to yawn. "The giant kitchen tent will be there until New Year's Eve morning, so I figured any positive publicity for The Park Inn couldn't hurt. Morbid curiosity over recent events has kept the place packed regardless, so it's not like we need it. I'm riding the notoriety train straight to the bank before it inevitably dries up, and we need another stunt. Turns out murder is as good for business as a record. Now, if you'll excuse me, I'm done with this farce."

With that declaration, Tristan slid out from the booth and strode towards the exit while Ryan stepped aside to let him pass. Victor also shambled unsteadily to his feet, staggering after Tristan. No one tried to stop his lumbering and silent departure.

Grant returned to the kitchen without looking back at the awkward void left behind. Elena rose from the booth, keen to extricate herself from the situation. Acting on instinct, Claire hurried after her into the snowy square, wanting to probe her further away from the others' influence; she was the only one who hadn't made Claire's skin crawl somehow.

"I'm sorry, I need to get to work now," Elena said as Claire caught up to her on the edge of the market. "My shift starts soon."

"I'll walk with you," Claire offered, sensing she was on the cusp of a revelation with the quiet woman. "It's only around the corner. Bought these jeans there last year. Only cost me a couple of quid."

"Oh." Elena looked down and offered a smile. "They fit you well."

They set off together down the narrow lane leading away from the main square. As they passed Marley's Café and the small gallery, Claire watched Elena shrink into herself, shoulders stooped inside her coat as she avoided eye contact.

While Elena unlocked the shop, Claire asked, "I thought you quit?"

"Changed my mind. Just a bad day at work. Stress got

to me. With everything going on with Grant and Marco…"

"And *what* happened between you, Grant, and Marco? I feel like there are still pieces missing."

Elena kept her gaze fixed on the keys, her hands shaking. They slipped from her grasp, so Claire darted to get them. She pushed the key into the shop's lock and twisted, and Elena gave her a grateful smile.

"I *did* love Grant," she said, pushing the door to the dark second-hand clothes shop. They stepped inside, where it smelled pleasantly of pot-pourri and mothballs. "The breakup blindsided me. Yes, Marco did catch my eye when we first met—he could be quite captivating. But I never would have *dreamed* of leaving Grant for him. The thought that you can't find someone else attractive just because you're spoken for is… archaic. It was a primal thing, that's all. Like when a nice new coat comes in, or I see some art I adore next door." She exhaled, wincing as though she regretted that 'primal thing.' "After the split, with my heart broken, Marco was suddenly... *there*. So attentive and charming initially, I couldn't help but fall in love. I didn't think I was rebounding, but I must have been. That lovely fuzzy feeling faded so quickly. It flicked off like a switch when he announced he would break that record. That became his new love. It's like he *had* me, so he put me on the back burner."

Elena beckoned Claire behind the counter to the

computer under the desk. After it took an age to load, she scrubbed through the camera feed covering the front door and let it play. The dated footage showed Elena straightening a clothing rack before leaving the shop at 6:39 p.m. on Christmas Eve—almost ten minutes after Marco's estimated time of death.

"I knew it was later," Elena stated as she switched the monitor off again. "I know you suspected me when we spoke in the tent that day, but I could never..." Her voice broke. "Marco broke my heart differently, but I'm no killer, Claire."

"I know," Claire said, offering a smile. "And for what it's worth, I didn't suspect you much then, either." She hesitated, debating her next question. "What about Grant? When I asked you who you thought could have killed Marco and Grant came in, you gave Mo Farah a run for his money with how fast you got out of there. Do you think Grant was capable of killing Marco?"

Elena looked thoughtful as she chose her words. "Grant has been through a *lot* lately, outside of all the business with Marco. The week before he ended things between us, his beloved Nan died."

"Oh, I... I didn't know," Claire said, a lump growing in her throat. "He spoke about her. How she passed on her love of cooking to him."

"He'd go to see her three times a week without fail." She smiled, looking off into the distance. "Even when she wouldn't remember him, and I could see it tearing him up, he never missed a visit. He would make her all her favourites. Sometimes, it would bring her back like the tastebuds could remember what the mind couldn't." She blinked back tears, shaking her head. "He never *once* lost his temper or even raised his voice when we were together. The Grant *I* knew was a real sweetheart. But his Nan's death *changed* him..."

This revelation surprised Claire, who had thus far seen only Grant's arrogant, volatile side. "That's helpful context. Thank you, Elena. There's something else... I overheard you with Grant in the pub. He was discouraging you from going to the police?"

Elena nodded. "Because I knew that with all his public fights and our tangled history, Grant would immediately be suspect number one in their eyes. Instead of making assumptions, I wanted them to learn the full story about our relationship and break up directly from *us*. I was trying to help, honestly. But Grant didn't see it that way. He thought it would make us look suspicious, so I held back." She snapped on a smile when the door opened, and a woman strolled in, going straight for the racks. "Look, I need to get to work."

"Me too," Claire said, nodding her thanks. "Say no more. I'll see you around."

Claire left Elena feeling somewhat unsettled by this new information about the usually cocky Grant's potential vulnerability. However, she wasn't sure if his nan's recent death ruled him out as Marco's vicious killer.

Ryan had followed in her shadow, though he was waiting outside the gallery, gazing at the artwork in the front window. He appeared lost in thought, his hands shoved into his pockets as he peered closer. She cleared her throat, and he stepped back.

"Getting inspired for your next creation?"

Ryan gave her a sheepish grin, abandoning his studious air. "Just keeping an eye on this alley until you emerged safely. You never know when someone might strike you down around here these days."

Claire smiled, touched by his protective nature, even if it was unnecessary. She stood on tiptoes to plant a grateful kiss on his chilled cheek. "I'm so lucky to have you, Ryan."

"I think I'm the lucky one, Claire." He returned the kiss. "I can't bear the thought of anything happening to you. Did you manage to learn anything useful from Elena?"

Claire huddled into his warmth as they made their way across the square. "A few bits, but I'll tell you later. I need to get back to the shop. I've left Damon alone far too much lately, and with the speed he's been going through the graphic novels he keeps buying from the stall across from us in my absence, I'm going to have to double his wages."

They parted at the market, and before it vanished around the corner, Claire looked off to The Park Inn. Even with Elena officially ruled out, she was still no closer to uncovering the truth, but the one thing she did know for sure was that interviewing Grant, Tristan, and Victor had only made them seem all the guiltier.

CHAPTER SEVENTEEN

*L*ater that afternoon, an hour before closing, Claire hurried around the candle shop, tidying up shelves and restocking displays after a whirlwind of shoppers had turned the place upside down. All but four of the frosted plum candles had been sold, and no other festive scents were left on the shelves.

As busy as she'd been since her group interview at the pub, she couldn't stop turning over the case details in her mind. She kept circling back to one suspect in particular —Grant. Of all of them, his volatile temper seemed most likely to erupt in violence.

"With Leslie getting her job back at the pub and wanting to give the record another go, it makes sense," Claire said to Damon when they were finally alone after the last customer stopped her twenty-minute browsing without buying a thing. "Grant wanted that head chef job. He only recommended Marco because he knew Marco would hire him. Grant wasn't going to stand by to drag along more deadwood when he'd, in his words, 'finally got what he deserved.'"

"And Leslie got what *she* deserved?" Damon said, flipping the sign on the door. "I suppose it did happen behind the pub. You said there was a door that led out there."

"From kitchen to alley in a few steps."

"And trauma does do strange things to people," Damon continued, nodding in agreement. "I've been thinking more about what you said about Grant's nan dying. That kind of sudden loss can unmoor a person like nothing else. My Uncle Martin shaved his head and joined a transcendental meditation group in India when his wife died." He dropped into the chair behind the counter and reached for his *Doctor Who* graphic novel. "Came back after a week because it was too hot. We were never allowed to talk about it."

"*Almost* like murder then," Claire agreed, kicking an empty cardboard box into the storeroom, "in that it's *nothing* like murder."

"It was murder to my eyes that he still wore the robes for months after. Man didn't know how to wrap the things. I'm still scarred from the eyefuls I'd get when he bent over to pick up the post in the morning." He flipped open the book and put his feet on the counter with a shudder. "The point is that grief can make normal people behave in ways they never normally would. Elena said Grant was placid before his Nan died, then all of a sudden, he's screaming in a kitchen and waving a knife in *your* face. You're right. What's to say he didn't stab Marco in the back and bash Leslie's brains in?"

Claire paused her tidying, chewing her lip, suddenly unsure of her theory. "If anything, you'd think the grief would leave him too drained to do all that?"

"Think about how loopy we get in this shop when we've both had too little sleep for a few days." He glanced over his glasses with a playful smile. "If the cameras in this place were streaming online, we'd either become overnight stars or sectioned."

"Good point," she said, tapping his feet off the counter so she could wipe it down. "I suppose everyone handles death differently. When my grandad died, I just cried a lot."

"The *normal* response," he agreed with a nod. "Shaving your head and moving to India or reaching for the knives and bricks? *Abnormal* response."

"You're right, and I just can't get it out of my head that it *has* to be Grant," Claire insisted, returning to cleaning already spotless jars with a feather duster. "Something about his arrogant, mocking attitude just feels... unhinged. He even made a joke about Leslie haunting the pub, and it hadn't even been twenty-four hours since she was murdered. There's this feeling that he could lash out at any moment."

"Well, I trust your sleuthing instincts," Damon replied, saving his page with his finger. "Just... be careful if you plan to confront him. Grief mixed with a temper can be a volatile combination, and look what happened last time. No wonder Ryan's become your unofficial bodyguard." Resuming his reading, he added, "Besides, Grant could have always been like that, and Elena was looking at him through rose-tinted glasses. She said herself she fell for Marco's charm, and…"

But Claire was no longer listening, her restless momentum building as conviction coursed through her. After the group interview at the pub, she felt *confident* Grant had to be the one who had brutally murdered both Marco and Leslie in fits of jealous rage.

And she was going to get him to confess, whatever it took.

Grabbing her coat off the rack in the storeroom, Claire burst out the back door in a gust of icy air. She moved with renewed purpose along the back alley as the streetlamps flickered to life in the dusk, casting the village in an otherworldly glow. Icicles clung to eaves and glinted down at Claire like jagged teeth as she passed.

"Claire, wait up!" Damon called, jogging after her,

bundled up in his coat. "Where are you dashing off to so urgently?"

Claire kept up her brisk pace towards The Park Inn without slowing. "I'm going to confront Grant before I lose my nerve. I know it was him, Damon. I can feel it in my gut."

"Just give me a minute, I'll close up the shop, and—"

"I need to catch him before the dinner rush. Close up without me. I'll be back soon."

"Claire, it might not be safe to—" Damon pleaded, halting his pursuit as the distance between them widened. "Try not to get stabbed. Or bricked."

"Promise I won't."

Outside The Park Inn, Claire considered walking through the front entrance. The dinner rush was in full swing, and she wasn't sure a second attempt at worming her way into the kitchen would work a second time. Inhaling a deep breath, the icy air needled at her throat and lungs, but she embraced the discomfort, letting it sharpen her focus. Doubling back, she followed the path around the back of the pub.

Claire paused, gazing at the spot where Leslie's body had been just days before. The cobblestones had been scrubbed clean, not a trace of blood remaining. But in Claire's mind, even though she hadn't seen Leslie's body in situ, the image of Leslie's crumpled form lingered like a ghost.

"Hope she doesn't end up haunting the place," Claire repeated aloud, Grant's cold joke echoing around her mind. "It *must* be him."

If only Leslie had lived to go her own way, find her path and purpose beyond chasing fleeting glory in her father's shadow. Perhaps she could have opened her restaurant or returned to college like she'd suggested in the pub—anything but dying alone in a frozen alleyway, her dreams dashed and unfulfilled.

Claire mourned for the woman Leslie could have grown to be if fate had not intervened so cruelly. She wished Leslie's restless spirit peace, wherever it may linger. With a heavy sigh, Claire stepped over the spot the brick had been and went to the back door.

Watery light filtered out through the small circular window into the gleaming kitchen. The aromatic, yeasty scent of baking bread wafted from inside, where Grant conducted his crew like a captain running a tight ship. Still, he didn't raise his voice—didn't wave a knife in anyone's face.

Even Mr Hyde had Dr Jekyll.

Claire waited, lingering in the shadows, as one of the younger chefs left his station and slipped out the back door for a cigarette break. As he passed, he paused and asked if Claire had a light. She patted her pockets apologetically, despite knowing she didn't have one.

"There's a shop just around the corner, next to the estate agent's," she pointed out.

The chef looked back at the kitchen with a sigh, snatching the cigarette from his lips. He wedged a brick in the slowly closing back door to keep it open and set off at a light jog. After the chef disappeared from view, Claire hesitated, unsure whether to confront Grant. Hardening her nerves, she slipped inside, the savoury aroma of simmering vegetables encasing her.

No sooner had she entered the kitchen than she collided straight into Grant's hurrying form. A large pot slipped from his grip and landed on the tiles, sending tomato soup up in a volcanic eruption between them. Claire jumped back as dots of the hot soup splashed against her face. Grant's chef whites absorbed the most of it.

"*Claire...*" Grant gritted his teeth, and Claire braced herself for a split second as his hands clenched by his sides, half-expecting him to lash out violently. "Well, isn't that just *perfect?*"

"Grant, I'm sorry, I—"

"Shouldn't be in here?" he bit before letting out an irritated huff as he glared down at his soaked chef's whites. "Good job. It was on its way to the bin anyway. Too much salt. What do you want, Claire? I'm busy." He handed her a tea towel and added, "Are you alright? It was quite hot."

"I... I'm fine."

She dabbed at her face, stunned by how calmly Grant was taking the mess she'd caused in his kitchen. But she couldn't let herself get distracted from why she was there. Her theory *did* make sense.

"Have you got a moment?" she asked, nodding at the back door. "This shouldn't take long."

"I have a soup to make from scratch, and..." Sighing, he looked around the kitchen as his crew watched on in interest. "Johnson, get those tomatoes sliced up, double speed, and Michelle, I want a pot sizzling with garlic and onions in the next thirty seconds. And will *someone* ring that service bell again? Those plates for table four have been sitting there for three minutes. That steak will go from medium rare to medium under those hot lamps." Reaching around Claire, he yanked open the back door and gave her a gentle shove outside. "You have *one* minute."

Out in the alley, the young chef who'd run off for a lighter returned, though when he saw Grant, he doubled back and lit up around the corner. Claire inhaled a deep breath, the scent of cigarette smoke wafting past her. She wouldn't beat around the bush if she genuinely had one minute.

"I know it was you, Grant," she said, locking eyes with the head chef. "*You* killed Marco. And Leslie, too."

Grant slowly arched a brow, his surprise shifting into

amusement. He let out a derisive snort. "What is this? I think you've watched one too many police dramas." He shook his head, placing a hand on the back door. "Don't be so daft, Claire. Why the hell would I kill either of them and ruin my career in the process?"

"I *know* it was you." Thrown off-guard by Grant's nonchalance, Claire faltered. She cleared her throat and tried again, infusing her voice with more conviction. "B-because you were jealous. Both professionally and romantically. Marco stole your ideas and your spotlight as head chef. And he stole Elena from you, too."

Grant pulled his palm back from the door. He crossed his arms and leaned against the wall, regarding Claire with a mixture of amusement and pity with a tilted head.

"Is that right?" he said with a sigh. "Hate to shatter your sleuthing delusion, but I never gave a toss about any of that. I'm the one who dumped her, remember?" He laughed, looking utterly unconcerned. "Face it—you've got *no* proof, only wild accusations. So quit wasting my time unless you'll pay my hourly wage."

Striving to regain the upper hand, Claire took a step closer and directly met Grant's scornful gaze. "I know you have a temper and could easily have lashed out in a jealous rage. Your arrogant attitude screams unhinged resentment towards Marco for eclipsing you."

Grant's mouth curved into an icy, taunting smile that sparked an instinctive unease in Claire's gut.

"Everybody thinks they know me so well, don't they?" he remarked, pushing off the wall to slowly advance towards her. "Grant with the out-of-control ego and temper. Have you never had a bad day at work? Never said—*done*—things in the heat of the moment you regret?"

"Like murder?"

"Like *shouting*, you halfwit," he snapped, clenching his eyes. "Like pointing that knife at you. I knew it was one of the dumbest things I could have done then, but you're just so... *irritating*."

"Now you sound like my mother."

Grant surprised her by laughing. He reached into his pocket and, after some tapping, thrust his phone screen in her face, inches from her nose. Squinting at the bright display, she could make out Grant's employee portal, with a digital timestamp that clearly showed he had clocked into work at 6:22 p.m. on Christmas Eve—just minutes into the window of Marco's estimated time of death.

"You're probably going to say that I stabbed him and somehow worked my way through the crowd and got here to clock in, all in under two minutes," he said. "Or that I clocked in and went off to stab him, but neither is true. I stayed here, working the dinner shift, while Marco put all his attention on that stupid record as he had been for weeks. I would have loved to have seen the back of him, but I didn't kill him. Or Leslie."

He slowly lowered the phone, his flat grey eyes boring into Claire's as the incriminating timestamp cemented her mistake.

"Happy?" he muttered. "Now, I have a soup to finish. Stop wasting my bloody time."

Claire's legs wobbled, uncertainty and embarrassment flooding her. How could she have been so wrong? She thought of the digital timestamp again—an irrefutable alibi.

Desperate to repair her botched, impulsive accusation, she stammered, "I-I'm so sorry, I shouldn't have assumed. It's just... with your past with Elena and your issues with Marco—"

"Don't try to dig your way out of this," he interjected, pushing open the back door. "If I wanted the arrogant sod gone for good, you think I'd cook up some wild goose chase to stab him outside surrounded by witnesses? Could've easily slipped something nasty into his dinner any night I felt like it if I wanted him dead, and believe me, it crossed my mind, but…" His words trailed off, and he looked off through the pub; Claire was sure he was looking towards Still Loved. "Doesn't matter anymore. Please leave me alone, Claire. And *Jones*?" he yelled in the direction of the cigarette smoke, "I said you could have a few puffs. Get your behind back into the kitchen."

The young chef hurried around the corner, tossing the half-finished cigarette to the cobbles. The door swung shut behind them both, and staring at the fizzling embers of the lit tip, Clair shrank beneath the weight of her own mortification. Of course, slipping something toxic into Marco's meal would have been far easier and more discreet. What had she been thinking, blurting out such a reckless, baseless accusation? The truth was she had no real evidence of Grant's guilt at all—just circumstantial dislike for his arrogance, and after too many hours cooking up theories at the shop, she'd foolishly let her emotions override logic.

Trudging back out into the cold clarity of the dark square, Claire moved in a discouraged daze back around the corner to the alley behind her shop, the certainty she'd left with crumbling to utter self-doubt.

Could she trust any of her instincts about the other suspects? She'd wrongly put Malcolm Richards in the frame. Perhaps she'd got Victor and Tristan all wrong as well, and there was another suspect running around the village without a question mark above their head.

Stepping back into the shop, she avoided meeting Damon's eyes, humiliation still burning through her.

"Sorry I rushed off like that," she mumbled, scanning over the day's takings on the till roll, the tiny words and numbers blurring into nothingness. "Turns out I didn't think things through properly."

Damon paused his sweeping. "What happened? Did Grant—"

"No, he didn't do anything wrong," she said. "Alibi. And a strong one, at that. I'm the one who made a mistake... a really stupid, reckless mistake."

"It's okay to be wrong, Claire," Damon said. "I overcharged Mrs Monsoon double this morning, and she still hasn't been back to have a go at me yet. You still have other suspects."

Claire nodded half-heartedly, wishing she could believe they would ultimately untangle the messy ingredients of this plum pudding disaster. But her conviction had been punctured, leaving her directionless among too many knotted and frayed possibilities.

"Other suspects," she agreed, hitting the button on the till to empty the contents, "for the police to sift through. I'm tapping out of this fight, and it was never mine to begin with."

CHAPTER EIGHTEEN

*C*laire and Ryan strolled arm-in-arm down the quiet lane. Passing the small art gallery between Marley's Café and the second-hand shop, Claire paused, struck by inspiration.

"Want to pop inside for a gander?" she asked, nodding at the window displaying colourful abstract art. "Might help clear our heads."

Ryan hesitated. Something conflicted in his eyes before he managed a smile. "Sure, why not."

As they wandered between the abstract paintings and sculptures, Claire paused before a watercolour seascape. Letting her eyes drift closed, she found herself transported back in time. The tasteful gallery vanished, replaced by the warm, elegant interior of Victor's restaurant in its heyday. White tablecloths and flickering candles covered every surface, the quiet music drowned out by the energetic hum of conversation. Waiters in crisp white shirts hurried about delivering heaping plates of exquisitely plated plum puddings. Near the kitchen doors, a younger Victor surveyed his domain, his full head of auburn hair impeccably styled. His eyes were bright, but his smile appeared tense as he scrutinised each table. Claire imagined him snapping his fingers, demanding perfection from his harried staff. His controlling presence dominated the atmosphere.

With a shake of her head, Claire opened her eyes, returning to the peaceful present-day gallery. Victor's legacy remained, though nothing more than an echo. Claire caught up to Ryan as he peered closely at an abstract painting.

"Reminds me of your mum's work," she said.

Ryan's smile turned wistful. "She really was incredible. Anything I know, I got from her. I can copy her style, but I'll never have her raw talent."

Claire turned him gently, meeting his eyes. "You have talent of your own. Your Christmas cards have almost all sold."

"Because they're cute and festive, that's all."

"Because of *your* art." She squeezed his hands. "I wish you could see your potential like I do. You could be selling in galleries like this one day."

Ryan sighed. "You've always believed in me, Claire.

Even when I didn't believe in myself. Even when we were kids, I worried about every brushstroke and colour choice for my GCSE coursework."

"Because you're special, Ryan Tyler. I've always seen that."

He drew her close, staring at a watercolour of Northash's square from a sunny summer day. "The prices here are insane, and my work isn't *that* far from the quality of this stuff."

"Better, I'd say. If you did sell more paintings, we'd be closer to that deposit *if* we got our own place."

"*When.*"

"When." She smiled, picturing the home Ryan dreamed of for them both, with the garden for the kids. "Who knows what the new year will bring? Maybe a few more paintings that make it out of your cellar, eh?"

Ryan smiled, gallery spotlights catching gold flecks in his eyes. "You're becoming my manager."

"Deal." She winked. "I'll take my commission in cuddles."

Back outside in the softly falling snow, spirits lifted, Claire looped her arm through Ryan's. But as they turned towards The Park Inn, doubt crept back. She thought of her botched accusation of Grant, the tangled threads of mystery still surrounding Marco's murder. She'd spent most of the day trying to distract herself, but the case was never too far away.

Noticing her change in mood, Ryan stopped. "What's wrong?"

She sighed, shoulders slumping. "I made such a mess of things with the investigation. Accusing Grant with no proof? I don't know what I was thinking."

"One mistake doesn't mean you should give up. I know how tenacious you are. It's one of the reasons I love you." He tucked a windswept strand of hair behind her ear. "You just have to believe in yourself, like *I* believe in you. Like you keep telling me how I should believe in myself."

"I don't know..."

"Claire, you're the most resilient person I know. If you set your mind to solving this, I *know* you will." He smiled wide. "We spend half our time teaching the kids it's okay to be wrong sometimes. What matters is picking yourself up again."

Claire knew he was right, but she wasn't sure it was that simple. Picking herself up after her disastrous confrontation with Grant would require an industrial-strength crane.

"Said I'd nip to the cul-de-sac. Fancy tagging along? Not sure I feel like facing my mother alone."

"I said I'd meet Em in the pub for dinner with the kids, but if you—"

"You enjoy your night," she assured him. "Not sure it'll be much fun for them tonight. I think my dad wants to talk about the case. I'll pop by yours on the way home. Better set off now before my mother sends out a search party."

"I don't want you walking to your parents alone when—"

"I'll be fine." She stood on tiptoes for a quick kiss. "I'll see you later, I promise. You should pick out the piece you want to submit to the gallery. Those cards have almost all sold. I *am* going to win that bet, and you *are* going to submit something to that place."

"Same to you, too," he said, waving her off. "As much as I want you to be safe, Claire, don't give up on yourself just yet."

CLAIRE LEANED AGAINST THE SMOOTH MARBLE ISLAND OF her mother's pristine kitchen, mechanically stirring her black coffee. She was avoiding her mother's examining gaze, wishing she had the full strength of her shop's coffee machine instead of instant.

"Honestly, Claire, what were you thinking charging in there alone to confront that maniac after he tried to *stab* you?" Janet said as she aggressively scrubbed at a casserole dish in the sink. "You could have followed that Leslie into an early grave. The same alley, too! He would only have had to reach out and grab a brick…"

"Alright, Janet," Greta snapped from the dining table where she was playing cards with Claire's father. "The girl gets the message."

As grateful as Claire was that Granny Greta was there to balance things out, she'd hoped talking out the confrontation with Grant with her family would provide some perspective, but her mother's criticism only amplified her doubts.

"Your mother is just worried for your safety, little one," her offered, folding his hand. "Perhaps going alone wasn't the wisest course of action, given his history."

"I know, I know, it was reckless and stupid," Claire muttered, leaning back against the counter and blowing ripples across the steaming surface of her coffee. "For as convinced as I was that Grant was the killer, he did turn out to be innocent." She sighed, shaking her head. "Some detective I'm turning out to be. Good job I'm not trying to get on the force, right?"

"Oh, dear," Janet moaned, clattering the casserole dish onto the draining board. "After all those years of sleepless nights with your father, I don't think I could stand that again." Drying her hands on a towel, she added, "Besides, I don't think you got good enough grades in school to pass the admission, dear."

"Claire could be running that station if she wanted," Greta cried, glaring at Janet while she shuffled the deck. "A damn better sight than

Ramsbottom, that's for sure. This nasty business has everyone rattled, so don't be so hard on yourself. Ramsbottom wouldn't have half a case if you hadn't conducted all those interviews for him. That man is bone idle."

"At least we can agree on something, Greta," Janet said, toasting her cup of tea across the room. "Harry has never been more distracted. It's like he thought he could sail through to next year with his feet up."

"If only criminals worked to the holiday schedule," Alan said. "And your granny is right, Claire. Don't be so hard on yourself. I couldn't count how many wrong accusations I made over my career. Don't give up yet, little one."

Janet looked less convinced as she continued going through the washing up. "Small mercies, I say. There have been two brutal murders already. Perhaps it's best to let the police handle the rest, dear."

The toilet of the downstairs bathroom flushed, and DI Ramsbottom squeezed himself out, wiping his damp hands on his shirt. He helped himself to more biscuits from the kitchen counter before resuming his place at the kitchen table.

"Where are we up to? New game?" He brushed crumbs from his tie and cleared his throat. "Ah, Claire. When did you get here?"

"Ten minutes ago," Claire said, glancing at the

downstairs bathroom door, wondering how long he'd been in there. "Any case updates?"

"I was hoping to ask you the same."

Granny Greta gave Claire an 'I told you so' roll of her eyes as she split the deck three ways. Gripping her steaming mug, she joined them at the table, and Greta threw some cards in front of her. While Greta finished the dealing, Claire filled Ramsbottom in on her Grant confrontation.

"Ah, yes," Ramsbottom muttered through a mouthful of gingerbread biscuits. "I should have mentioned that I'd confirmed Grant's alibi. Elena's too. Still trying to track down Tristan's personal trainer at his fancy pants private gym, but his secretary said his trainer was on a tropical island filming 'content' for his 'feed', whatever that means."

"Another round of Rummy?" Greta announced.

"I have a better idea," Ramsbottom interjected, lifting his briefcase onto the table. "Perhaps we should go back over the case files instead, just one more time?" He popped up the briefcase, revealing a stack of paperwork.

Claire sipped her cooling coffee. "I looked at everything on that USB drive ten times already. Just keep going in circles."

"Oh, let's toss those dusty old papers on the fire and be done with it," Janet said, bringing over her handheld vacuum. "This case is giving me a headache." She flicked

FROSTED PLUM FEARS

on the vacuum and began sucking up Ramsbottom's crumbs.

Alan held up a hand. "It wouldn't hurt to give the files *one* more look, would it? Sometimes, a fresh set of eyes helps shake things loose. What do you say, little one?"

Unsure, Claire glanced at Granny Greta, seeking her decisive vote, and Greta waved a hand dismissively, gathering up the playing cards. "We can play Rummy any night. There's still a killer out there somewhere, and who knows who they'll target next? That's what matters most."

Knowing Granny Greta was right, Claire reluctantly conceded. "Okay, fine. One more time through the files it is."

Ramsbottom tipped his briefcase upside down and spread the case notes out on the table. Janet huffed, wafting her hand before returning to the kitchen. After sorting through, Alan separated the paperwork into suspect piles, taking Grant for himself. Claire split the Victor pile with Greta while Ramsbottom went over Tristan's pile.

"You know I never trusted that man after the way he sacked me," Granny remarked.

"I never knew he fired you," Claire said

"I told him exactly where he could stick those plums!" Greta cried, slamming her palm on the table. "He tried to send me off to Kent on the *bus* on some wild goose chase errand when his local stockist couldn't find those damn Damsons."

Alan chuckled. "I'll never forget *that* night."

"Me neither," Janet called from the kitchen. "Though, you didn't need to flip that table, did you, Greta?"

"It's been thirty years. Let it go!" Greta called back before turning to Claire. "And to be honest, love, I was glad to be clear of that place. He did me a favour, firing me. Nothing but a hotbed of drama and tantrums working under a man like that."

As Greta continued reminiscing about her defiant exit, Claire carefully withdrew the recipe drafts they'd found amongst Marco's possessions. She angled the papers under the overhead light, squinting at the indentation marks Ramsbottom had pointed out back in the giant kitchen tent.

"Harry, did you ever get these pencil etchings properly analysed?" she asked.

"Ah, no." Ramsbottom's cheeks turned a shade as deep as a plum. "Afraid that slipped my mind after we left the tent. So much on my mind. But I'll get the experts on it first thing."

"Oh, for heaven's sake," Janet muttered. She yanked open a kitchen drawer and grabbed a pencil and pad of paper. Before Ramsbottom could protest, she used the edge of the pencil to shade the paper on top of the recipe draft, rubbing lightly. When she held the page up triumphantly to the glow of the lights wrapped around the Christmas tree, the indented writing was revealed. "Never written a phone number down on the hallway notepad and then had your husband rip the top page off for his case notes?"

"That was *also* thirty years ago, dear," Alan said, kissing Janet on the cheek as he joined her at the tree. "Is that a phone number?"

Peering closer, Claire saw the numbers, but it wasn't a phone number. They were quantities. A nearly identical recipe to the first one she'd just pulled from the evidence bag. Except for the etchings, the quantities were different. Only the ingredient amounts differed and increased slightly from Marco's version.

"Same recipe but modified," Claire said, pulling up Marco's version. "2550 kg of chopped candied peel and chopped spiced Damson plums to the other versions 2500 kg. 102 kg of mixed spices to the 100 kg. 27 kg of ground ginger to and 25 kg."

"Almost the same," Ramsbottom said. "Wouldn't make a difference at that size, would it?"

"Marco's plum pudding weighed was further from the tonne than Victor's." The answer struck Claire. "Misdirection. Remember, Tristan said Victor was advising Marco initially, and Leslie told me Victor pulled back when he realised Marco was using him for publicity.

Victor was offended that Marco didn't want him to help, side by side."

"But Victor still gave him his recipe," Greta pointed out. "Or why would Marco bother using Damson plums specifically?"

"This must have been Victor's attempt to sabotage the recipe so Marco would fail," Claire thought aloud. "Marco was so arrogant. He would have thought he'd won the lottery being able to cut corners like that."

Alan tapped his chin. "Grant mentioned in his statement that Victor often stole his recipe ideas and passed them off as his own. This rewritten version would allow Victor to retain the glory if Marco got as far as he did."

"Yet Marco's final pudding weighed even less than Victor's record attempt," Ramsbottom mused. "So, Victor only tweaked the recipe *slightly* to avoid detection. But it was enough to doom Marco's attempt. Well, I'd say he has to be our—*my*—top suspect now."

"I'd have to agree, Detective," Claire said, her mouth suddenly dry. "With his history of aggression and obsession over that record..."

She trailed off as Ramsbottom held up a hand. "Victor was drowning his sorrows at the Hesketh not an hour ago before I came here. Wasn't in the best way, and..." His eyes widened as he gasped. "The *plum* skin!"

"Plum skin?" Alan echoed.

"Under Leslie's nails," he said, shaking his head. "I forgot to say. It wasn't human skin from a bruise, it was skin from a plum. Like she'd been wrestling with a plum moments before she died."

"Victor had plums on him. Ryan smelt them when he talked to him in the bathroom." Claire shot to her feet, grabbing her coat. "I need to speak with Victor before the alcohol erases his memory completely for the night."

"So much for *quitting* the case!" her mother called after her.

But all thoughts of quitting vanished as Claire hurried out the door before anyone could object. She had to confront Victor while this new revelation was fresh before he wandered off into the night.

CHAPTER NINETEEN

*T*he snowfall had stopped, leaving behind a hushed stillness over the village. Up ahead, golden light spilt from the windows of The Hesketh Arms, casting a soft glow across the otherwise deserted square.

Inside, cheerful chatter and laughter filled the pub. Claire scanned the crowd, noting familiar faces gathered around tables nursing pints or sipping mulled wine. In the far corner, she spotted Ryan seated with Em and the kids, who were playing a game of Connect 4 amongst their empty dinner plates. For a moment, she longed to join them, but she had more pressing business first.

Beside her, DI Ramsbottom rocked up onto his toes, craning his neck to peer over the crowd. "Blast it! He was right *here* at the bar."

Claire moved towards the bar, excuses already forming in her mind for why she was about to interrupt Malcolm and Theresa's evening. As she approached, Malcolm's expression soured, his earlier surliness at her accusation still simmering beneath the surface.

"I'm so sorry for suspecting you," Claire said in a rush. "I was completely wrong, and I never should have accused you. Of course, you weren't involved, Malcolm. I've been coming in here since I was a little girl, and you've never put a foot wrong."

Malcolm only grunted, but Theresa smiled kindly, ever the peacemaker. "No hard feelings, love. This whole mess has everyone on edge." She lightly elbowed her husband. "Right, dear?"

"Right," Malcolm grunted. "Apology accepted, I suppose."

"As a show of goodwill, a pint of homebrew," Theresa offered, already reaching for a glass. "On the house, of course."

"That's so kind of you, but I'm actually in a terrible rush at the moment." Claire's gaze darted around the pub. No sign of Victor anywhere. "It's quite urgent that I speak with Victor Michaels. Any chance you've seen him tonight? DI Ramsbottom said he was in here earlier?"

"Aye, he's been here for *hours*." Theresa leaning forward and said, "and between us, I'm going to cut him off when he gets out of the bathroom. He's been making quite the spectacle of himself."

From the end of the bar, Drunken Pete hiccupped loudly. "Making a right fool o' 'imself, more like. Been spoutin' the *craziest* stuff all night." He shook his head and took a long pull from his pint. "I always knew Victor had a few screws loose from his p-plum pudding obsession, but…"

Claire's heart raced as she edged closer to Pete. "What sort of crazy stuff exactly?"

Pete squinted at her, a wide, crooked grin spreading across his ruddy face. As pleased as he looked to see her, there wasn't a flicker of recognition in his eyes from their beer garden meeting only days ago. "Well, ain't ya a pretty thing. Got yourself a fella, lass?"

"She does." Ryan appeared at Claire's side, gently resting a hand on her back. "Everything alright? Thought you were going to your parents?"

"I did. I was, but we looked over the files again, and we found something…"

"*Sabotage!*" Ramsbottom whispered.

"And we're looking for Victor," Alan said, tapping his cane on the worn floorboards. "Evening Peter. It's been a while."

"As I live and b-breath," Pete said, squinting at Alan. "It 'as been a while, DI 'arris."

"Just Alan now," he said, patting his leg. "Retired. Hope you've given up the shoplifting, Peter."

"You were always the nicest o' them, sir," Pete said, holding up his palms and almost swaying off his chair in the process. "Scout's 'onour, I haven't nicked anythin' in years."

Ramsbottom cleared his throat loudly.

"Glad to hear it, Peter," Alan continued, moving in closer. "What sorts of 'crazy' things was Victor saying earlier."

"Ah, now, y'know 'ow some folks get when they've 'ad one too many." He drained his pint and held it up to Theresa with a nod, and she reluctantly started pouring him another. "People end up saying all kinds of nonsense."

"This pint is on me," Claire said, taking the pint before Theresa set it down. She placed it in front of Pete. "Call this my free one, Theresa. So, Pete? What kinds of things?"

Pete blinked slowly before bursting into raucous laughter. "Been jokin' 'bout 'getting away with murder' all night, but I 'aven't been taking the man seriously. Can't go believin' everythin' a drunk man spouts off about, can ya? I know ave talked some waffle in my time."

The bathroom door creaked open, and there he was. Victor stumbled out, blinking blearily under the lights until his gaze settled on their huddled group. Behind

Claire, she heard the efficient click of handcuffs as Ramsbottom prepared to apprehend his prime suspect.

But for as drunk as Victor was, he wasn't stupid.

He had, by his own admission, got away with murder.

He wasn't about to let himself get cuffed for it.

Victor sprinted towards the beer garden with unexpected speed, knocking past all the chairs and tables in his way. He slammed into the back door before he flung it wide open, slamming the wood into the wall behind it. Catching his balance, he disappeared into the night, the door banging shut behind him.

Ryan was off in a flash, bursting through the back door in pursuit. Claire stood rooted to the spot, groaning to herself for not following her very first instinct.

Her own words echoed back to her. All the way from Boxing Day when Damon had told her about overhearing Victor grumbling in the café about Marco stealing his legacy. And what had Claire said?

"Victor's motive couldn't be clearer," she repeated the words aloud. "I knew it from the start, and I let myself get so distracted by Grant and his temper."

"Don't blame yourself, little one," Alan assured her, clasping her hand. "Victor has been a slick one."

"Wait… so ya tellin' me…" Pete shook his head, banging a burp from his chest with a fist. "Victor actually *killed* that guy…"

"And probably his own daughter, too," Claire whispered. "I feel sick."

"So do I," Pete mumbled before charging off towards the bathroom.

Claire took his seat and took a sip of the untouched homebrew. Boxing Day... she'd had his cards marked on Boxing Day...

Moments later, Ryan returned empty-handed with an apologetic smile as he quickly caught his breath. "No sign of him out there. It's like he vanished into thin air."

"You were right, Ryan," she said, nodding at the bathroom door. "That recording you got when you bandaged up his hand. It *was* a confession."

Claire slumped against the bar, defeat washing over her despite Ramsbottom's assurances that Victor couldn't have gone far. After all her sleuthing, the actual murderer had slipped through her grasp at the final moment. She took a long sip from the pint Malcolm nudged closer.

"Chin up, Claire," he whispered. "If you went after him half as hard as you went after me, I know you tried your best."

But in the end, her best hadn't been good enough.

One last loose thread in this tangled case, and she'd let it unravel into the night.

CLAIRE SANK ONTO THE UPTURNED TERRACOTTA PLANT POT in her father's shed, the familiar earthy scents transporting her back to simpler times. But tonight, no nostalgic comfort could penetrate the bitterness settling upon her heart after Victor had slipped through her grasp yet again.

She stared sightlessly at the seed trays lined before her, replaying the scene from the pub over and over. Victor's stunned expression morphing to rage upon realising they'd put the pieces together. The electrifying moment their eyes locked, just before he bolted. Her leaden legs refusing to give chase quickly enough to stop him disappearing into the night.

The door creaked open and Ryan crouched beside her, his handsome face creased with concern.

"I'm annoyed, so I can't imagine how frustrating this must be for you," he said. "To come so close, only for Victor to run at the last second."

Claire sighed, the fight draining from her as she sagged against Ryan's sturdy frame. "I was right *there*, Ryan. If I'd just been a little faster..."

"You did everything you could," Ryan insisted, tilting her chin up to meet her eyes. "If only I'd been faster. I spent half my time at work moving quickly and he managed to get away. Because of *you* and your refusal to let this go, the police know Victor's guilty now. He can't hide forever. Not in this weather. He'll resurface."

"And if he doesn't?" Claire huffed out a cheerless laugh. "Victor might be a murderer, but he was clever enough to trick everyone around him. Clever enough to slip Ramsbottom's grasp more than once already."

She toyed with a packet of daffodil bulbs, thinking of the new beginnings those flowering trumpets would herald come springtime. Would Victor still be at large by then, a lingering shadow over their community? She looked to the small clock as hands slipped past midnight.

It was New Year's Eve.

So much for solving this by the New Year.

"You can't change the past, Claire. And your persistence brought us closer to the truth than anyone else could."

When she didn't look convinced, Ryan tried another track, his voice low and earnest. "You remember when we were teenagers, and you spent weeks teaching me to ride your bike no handed? And when I finally managed it, I got so cocky that I immediately crashed right into your father's prize rosebush?"

Despite herself, Claire huffed out a watery laugh at the memory. "I'd almost forgotten. Mum was furious for weeks over her 'Ruby Wedding' roses being decapitated. You almost broke your arm, too. She grounded me for a week for that one." She winked. "Worth it just to see you zooming around the cul-de-sac like that. Almost ran Mrs Beaton over in the process."

"I might never have gone for the rosebush if not for her cats... What I'm trying to say..." Ryan pulled her closer, his heartbeat steady beneath her cheek. "Is that we all make mistakes. Fall off the bike, so to speak. Even the best sleuths. But you can't let those falls define you, Claire. You have to get back on and keep pedalling towards the truth."

Claire let his wisdom penetrate the clouds enshrouding her, bolstering her faltering spirit. Ryan was right—she couldn't change the past. But the future still held possibility for revelations and justice, but not for her.

"This is the part where I say I'm going to get back on that bike, isn't it?"

"Say it then."

Heaving herself off the plant pot, Claire yanked on the chain and killed the light in the bulb above them. "It's Ramsbottom's bike now."

CHAPTER TWENTY

On the afternoon of New Year's Eve, the scents of lavender and rose tickled Claire's nostrils as she tinkered with formulas for her upcoming spring range. Though the little shop was packed for the final day of the 'Everything Must Go' sale, Claire had been hiding in the storeroom all morning. She'd been trying to get her mind as far away from anything festive. With the countdown to the new year underway, she was eager to fast forward to warmer days ahead.

These new formulas would never see the shelves.

She'd over-tinkered to the point where her nose was in a floral funk.

Each new blend more overpowering and indistinguishable than the last.

After Victor's narrow escape the evening before, Claire had been left with more questions than answers about the tangled threads connecting the record holder to the murders of Marco and Leslie. She added a final drop of rose oil into the formula before abandoning the attempt.

She'd revisit the range in the new year.

The tinkling of the shop bells announced a new arrival. Claire glanced into the shop to see Ryan ducking through the doorway, clad in gym clothes with a duffel bag slung over his shoulder.

"Early for lunch, isn't it?" Claire asked. "I thought you had back-to-back 'Spin into the New Year' classes today."

Ryan ran a distracted hand through his damp curls. "I do, but something... *odd* happened."

"Don't tell me," Damon interjected, handing over a bulging bag to a customer. "You saw Claire astral projecting herself onto a treadmill?"

Claire couldn't help laughing despite her mood as she gave his arm a light swat. But noting Ryan's uncharacteristic gravity, her humour quickly faded to unease.

"What did you see?" she asked quietly, leaning closer. Around them, customers chatted and pondered over displays, oblivious to the intensifying drama.

Ryan edged nearer, dropping his voice. "I was doing

my usual hourly sweep through the changing room and showers just to make sure nothing was going on back there." He shook his head, looking perturbed. "That's when I spotted Tristan having a pretty intense conversation with someone in the corner by the fire exit."

"Tristan?" Claire frowned. "Who was he talking to?"

"The man had his hood up and back to me, but I could see he had bushy, grey hair coming out the sides. And Tristan was talking to him in this low, tense voice, saying, 'Just meet me at the agreed place later on, and we'll get this sorted once and for all.'" His eyes locked onto Claire's, equal parts grave and electrified. "I think it might have been Victor he was talking to. Who else could it be?"

Implications whirled as puzzle pieces shifted into new configurations before her mind's eye. Victor and Tristan? The two of them had barely interacted outside of Tristan calling Victor sad for clinging to his record during their group interview. Victor had barely reacted to him at that moment.

The merry jangling of bells announced another new arrival. Claire looked up to see Ramsbottom stomping the snow from his boots.

"Any of those black cherry candles from the other year left?" he asked, scanning the shelves. "Mrs Ramsbottom can't get enough of them."

"As many as you want, Harry," Claire said, beckoning him closer. "Detective, you're not going to believe what Ryan just saw at the gym. Or should I say *who*?"

"Grey bushy hair," Ryan said, "talking to Tristan, and they arranged to meet later."

"*Tristan?*" Ramsbottom's brows shot up. "Bushy hair? You don't think…"

"Victor?" Claire finished, her mind whirring as much as Ramsbottom's must have been. "Could he be…?"

"You're certain it was Victor?" Ramsbottom hissed, pulling Ryan in with an arm around his broad shoulders. "Oh, very firm. And *moist*."

"Spin into the New Year classes," Damon said, squeezing Ryan's arm. "Crikey. They're so… *solid*. Don't let Sally get a feel of these. She'll be signing me up for the gym next."

"No chance it could be someone else?" Ramsbottom asked, still patting Ryan's arm. "No, but really… best keep Mrs Ramsbottom away, too. Good job you're a spoken-for man, Mr Tyler. So, Victor was in the gym?"

"Victor or a man who looked a *lot* like Victor," Ryan said, his cheeks blushing from all the attention. "And Tristan was talking to him in a secretive way. I checked the cameras before I came, but Tristan must have let him in through the back door."

"I'll call this in straight away and get officers combing

the area," Ramsbottom assured them, giving Ryan's arms one last pat before chuckling and shaking his head in disbelief. Clearing his throat, he pulled up his radio and ordered his officers to start searching the village at the gym. Between quick-fire instructions, he looked back at Ryan. "Did you catch any bits of their conversation? Any indication of what they were plotting?"

"Afraid not," Ryan admitted.

Ramsbottom nodded, finishing up his radio call.

"This reminds me of a classic *Doctor Who* scenario," Damon mused. All eyes turned to him. "Even the most sinister villains have their shadowy masters pulling the strings. Like Davros lurking behind the Daleks. What if Tristan is the real mastermind here and manipulated Victor into doing his dirty work?"

Ramsbottom frowned, tucking his radio away. "Victor had motive enough alone. But Tristan? He was owed all that money. Why would he want the man who owed him money dead?"

"Tristan *knew* he wasn't getting his money back," Claire said slowly as realisation crystallised. "At the big group interview, Tristan kept going on about how all the media coverage of the murder ended up benefitting The Park Inn regardless of the outcome... and he only gave Marco that money for publicity." She turned to Ramsbottom. "You were there, Detective. He said the pub was at capacity until the middle of January. He seemed to revel in it."

"We dug into his background," Ramsbottom said. "He had a lot of past financial trouble. If he was twenty grand down and knew Marco wouldn't pay it... he'd need to recoup that money somehow. A major PR boost to get back in the black." He nodded thoughtfully, bushy brows furrowing. "Debt can indeed be a powerful motivator. I believe you've given us some fresh, fruitful leads to pursue. My team will thoroughly interrogate Tristan immediately, and hopefully, we'll find Victor. If he's idiotic enough to still hang around, let's hope he shows up again."

With a courteous tip of his head, Ramsbottom headed back out into the cold, invigorated by this breakthrough development.

"Sounds like the game's still afoot to me," Damon whispered, serving a customer. "Your detective days are still over?"

"They were. Or so I believed after making such a mess of things." She heaved a conflicted sigh. "Only now, the closer we seem to get to the truth, the harder it is to just walk away."

Ryan gave her shoulder a supportive squeeze. "Well, for what it's worth, I think Northash still needs you, Claire. The truth won't unravel itself, even if Ramsbottom does seem to finally be sniffing the right trail. If Victor is still out there, and Tristan is pulling his strings, who knows what will happen next?"

The truth *was* still out there, awaiting discovery. And unless Ramsbottom could work a minor miracle, it seemed her detecting days weren't quite done yet after all.

"Time to get back on that bike?" she wondered.

CLAIRE SAT CURLED BY THE CHRISTMAS TREE OVERLOOKING the snowy back garden at the cul-de-sac, shredding a Christmas cracker crown. The remains of their dinner feast still cluttered the wooden table, forgotten in the wake of grimmer preoccupations.

Opposite her, Ramsbottom sat crumbling a slice of fruitcake between his fingers, looking rather dejected himself. After his high hopes surrounding the Victor sighting earlier that day, a thorough police sweep of the area around the gym had failed to turn up any trace of the missing murderer. It seemed Claire wasn't the only one feeling the bitter sting of disappointment as the year limped to its inglorious close.

Ramsbottom heaved a despondent sigh, sending a puff of powdered sugar drifting off the cherry atop his cake. "I was *certain* we'd collar Victor this time and wrap up this whole wretched business before the fireworks show. Now, the scoundrel remains at large to stir up who knows what manner of mischief in the new year."

Claire nodded gloomily. She had allowed herself a tiny flicker of hope that Ryan's sighting would be the break they needed to finally resolve the case, exactly one week after Marco's murder. But once again, the truth had slipped through her grasp like smoke.

"Chin up, you two," Alan said, clapping Ramsbottom on the shoulder before dropping into the seat beside him. "Tomorrow is a new year brimming with possibility, and Victor isn't the brightest bulb in the pack. He'll slip up somewhere, someday, and when he does, you can grab him. His face was all over the local lunchtime news bulletin." He shot Claire an encouraging smile. "His face was all over the local lunchtime news bulletin. You cracked the case. That's got to count for something, little one."

Ramsbottom didn't appear convinced as he picked at his cake crumbs, but Claire managed a small smile for her father's benefit. Ever the optimist, he refused to entertain even the notion of defeat. And though her own hope had dimmed to a mere flicker, she loved him all the more for fanning that fragile flame.

"I want to believe you, Dad," she said quietly. "It's just hard not to feel utterly useless with Victor still at large." She shook her head. "Especially when he already admitted his guilt to Drunken Pete, of *all* people."

At that moment, the kettle boiled to a finish, and Janet hurried over to lift it from its base. "Now, don't be so hard on yourself. You too, Harry." She poured the water into mismatched mugs. "You got close."

"But *no* cigar!" Ramsbottom sighed.

Janet brought the mugs over to the table before fixing Claire with a stern but loving look. "However, I do hope that after last time, you'll leave the policing to the professionals. This one felt far too dicey, dear. You want to make it to next year's Boxing Day sale, don't you? I passed by your shop earlier, and your shelves were bare!"

"All thanks to your banner, Mother. People have been asking if we're closing all week. Or so Damon has been telling me. I've barely been there." She stared down into the rising tendrils of steam from her coffee. "I suppose I'll be able to be more present at the shop when we reopen on the second."

"Might I propose a toast?" Alan ventured, raising his mug high. He waited until all eyes were upon him before declaring grandly, "Since the New Year is upon us... to possibility."

Chuckling, Ramsbottom lifted his own drink in solidarity. "To possibility! Let's hope we catch the scoundrel."

With soft, bittersweet smiles, Janet and Claire followed suit, clinking their mugs together over the crumb-strewn table. As she sipped the scalding coffee,

Claire allowed herself to embrace that delicate notion once more—*possibility*.

However slim, perhaps hope was not yet entirely lost.

———

CUTTING A BRISK PATH ACROSS THE SQUARE AS IT BEGAN TO fill with spectators securing early spots for the upcoming fireworks display, Claire made her way towards The Park Inn.

Following the scents wafting from the kitchen, Claire wound her way between the packed tables and chairs towards the door. Before the waiters could stop her, she pushed into the kitchen.

Amidst the billowing steam and the rhythmic chopping of knives, she spotted Grant working alone, spatula a blur as he scrambled a massive pan of eggs. Claire approached before nerves could stop her.

The cacophony of sizzling skillets and clattering pans masked her entrance. She cleared her throat until Grant glanced up from the stove, surprise shifting to irritation when he spotted her.

"You *again?*" He shook his head with a derisive snort. "Come to falsely accuse me of murder, have you? Or did you *really* enjoy your meal?"

Claire held up both hands. "No accusations, I promise. I actually came to apologise." She offered what she hoped was a disarming smile. "And to pick your brain about the missing knife, if you have a moment."

Grant eyed her warily for a tense moment before switching off the burner with a resigned sigh. "You've got thirty seconds."

"Then I'll make it quick," she said, inhaling a quick breath. "When I saw you lingering by the knife block the day before New Year's Eve in the kitchen tent... was the paring knife that killed Marco already missing?"

"That's *why* I was staring at the knife block. Marco, for all his faults, was very particular about where he put his things. Quite obsessive, actually."

"Makes sense," she said. "See either Tristan or Victor in the tent earlier that day?"

"I don't think Victor had any contact with Marco between Marco binning Victor off in the early stages and the old man trying to worm his way into the prep on record break day." Arching a brow, he folded his arms. "But Tristan? Yeah, he was there that morning. Demanding his money, like usual. Part of the reason Marco and I argued the day after. Amongst telling him I thought the quantities were all out of whack to reach the tonne, I told him he should never have borrowed the money for a stunt like that if he didn't intend to pay it back. Didn't like me 'messing with his head' so close to the record attempt, so he kicked me out."

"And you saw Tristan there before the knife went missing?

Grant thought about it for a moment before nodding. "Yeah, I think so. Why?"

Moving in close and already going over her thirty seconds, Claire told Grant her latest theory, and this time, the theory didn't include Grant's name once.

IN THE SQUARE WHERE THE FESTIVE MARKET HAD STOOD ON the day of Marco's murder, all the stalls had gone, as had the giant kitchen tent. Claire wandered the familiar yet strangely foreign space with Ryan, and Amelia and Hugo. She was still trying to process the dramatic events that had plunged their community into a week of chaos. Though the calendar was about to flip to the dawn of a fresh new year, there wasn't a resolution to be had.

"When are the fireworks?" Hugo asked.

"Midnight, dummy," Amelia said. "Like every year."

"Don't call your brother a dummy," Ryan pointed out. "But Amelia is right. Midnight, like last year."

"He fell asleep last year before it got to midnight," Claire reminded them.

Claire found herself compulsively scanning the square for any sign of the elusive Victor. Every man with long hair caught her eye. Every woman with grey hair, too.

Noticing her distant preoccupation, Ryan drew her in close.

"Don't beat yourself up too much over Victor slipping away. I could have seen wrong. It could have been someone else talking to Tristan in the gym."

Claire tried to mirror his encouraging smile, but it felt brittle and unconvincing. "I wish I shared your confidence. Time to finally give up?"

"Don't say that," piped up Amelia. "You'll catch that man."

Despite her bleak mood, Claire couldn't help but soften at the little girl's limitless faith. She gave Amelia's gloved hand an appreciative squeeze.

"You're very sweet. But I've made some big mistakes trying to solve this mystery."

"Everybody makes mistakes. That's how you learn," Hugo pronounced with the undeniable logic of a child. He sidled up and grabbed Claire's other hand, peering at her through the same open green eyes as his father. "You'll get him."

Sandwiched between the two optimistic children, Claire felt the first tender shoots of renewed hope take root within her.

"You've both raised some excellent points," she said. "How did you get to be so wise, eh?"

"It's all the ice cream," Ryan interjected, eyes twinkling. "Tubs and tubs of the stuff. Does wonders for expanding the mind."

Giggling, they released Claire's hands and ran over to their father, chanting, "Ice cream, ice cream!"

"Alright, you two, let's give Claire some peace and quiet. I'll treat you to sparklers and ice cream." He raised his eyebrows at Claire. "Unless you want to join us for a sugar overload?"

"For once, I'll pass on that offer." Claire waved them off. "I think I need some time alone with my thoughts before the New Year gets here."

As she watched them trek across the square, her heart swelled with gratitude. Their playful warmth had cut through the persistent chill of self-doubt plaguing her since Victor's disappearance. She reminded herself that goodness persevered, even amidst the longest shadows.

Turning slowly, Claire let her eyes roam over the familiar square, her gaze landing on the giant papier mâché plum in her window display. A giant ghost, the last lingering emblem of the muddled and fateful week that had changed everything. Even with none of the frosted plum candles left, she hadn't been able to bring herself to get rid of it.

If only she could turn back the clock.

She'd been so excited about the plum pudding hype back when the record-breaking event had seemed silly.

What she wouldn't give for silly.

A lone firework popped off in the distance near the

factory on the hill, and Claire turned to watch purple sparks glitter over the village. An hour early, but there was always someone who couldn't wait to ring the new year in. What Claire wouldn't give for more hours and days to put the case to bed. Sighing, she turned back to her shop, where the giant plum had captured the attention of a passer-by.

As she stared, the figure slowly turned, as if sensing her scrutiny. Claire glimpsed a mess of bushy grey hair escaping a crumpled cap. Her breath caught in her throat.

Before she could react further, another firework whistled high above from behind The Hesketh Arms, erupting in a dazzling crown of sparks that momentarily illuminated the square. Claire didn't turn around to look, but the man looking into her window did. She glimpsed Victor's rugged features in the flickering light as he turned and hastened away.

Claire looked for Ramsbottom, the police… anyone… but the crowd in the square had swallowed everyone up as midnight moved closer. She turned and watched as Victor slipped around the corner at the post office.

This was her chance, right here and now.

Claire broke into a sprint, keeping Victor's retreating figure in her sight as she pelted across the cobblestones. She wouldn't lose him again. Rounding the corner after him, she spotted Victor slipping behind The Park Inn pub up ahead. Perfect—a dead end. She pushed her burning legs faster, wishing she'd spent more time on the treadmill.

As the alley behind the pub came into view, Claire skidded to a halt, pressing herself flat against the brick facade to remain unseen. Peering cautiously around the corner, she saw Victor down the narrow lane, confronting none other than Tristan Raybourn himself. Claire's eyes widened. This had to be the promised meeting Ryan had overheard in the gym.

"You have to get out of Northash for good," Tristan was saying in a low, terse voice. "The police are combing every inch of this place looking for you, and I won't let you drag me down with you."

Despite the tension emanating from Tristan, Victor seemed bizarrely at ease, hands casually buried in his coat pockets. "Oh, keep your hair on; I just fancied seeing the fireworks tonight, for old times' sake. One last nostalgic hurrah before I disappear into the wind. My Wendy would never miss the fireworks. Would always say the new year was a chance for new beginnings."

Tristan's lips curled in contempt. "You sentimental old fool. This place will be glad to be rid of you. You're nothing but a washed-up has-been clinging to past glory, Victor Michaels."

Far from being insulted, Victor peered up at the inky night sky as more fireworks whistled and erupted somewhere in the park, bathing his lined face in a fleeting colour.

"Doesn't matter anymore, does it?" Victor sighed. "I lost everything but my record, so you're right. There's nothing for me here. We'll settle the small matter of payment, and I'll be on my way."

Clearly growing impatient with the old man's bizarre melancholy musings, Tristan brusquely shoved a stuffed duffel bag against Victor's chest. "Take this and disappear for good. No trains or planes. You might never be able to leave the country, and for heaven's sake, shave your head and keep it low. Disappear into the crowd."

"I'll live how I see fit."

"Whatever," Tristan huffed, retrieving another duffle bag from behind a beer barrel. "A little extra for you getting rid of Leslie, too. I never wanted to rehire her, but what else was I supposed to do? It would have been only a matter of time before she realised what Daddy had done."

Victor accepted the bag, but he continued to watch a shower of red and pink far off in the distance. "My daughter... I never meant... I..."

"Yeah, yeah, old man."

"I never meant to *kill* her," Victor hissed. "Getting rid of Leslie was *never* part of the deal. I never intended..." He trailed off, staring down at the bag dangling from his limp hands. When he spoke again, his voice was low and haunted. "I always tried to do what was best for her. Always tried to make her proud, but somewhere along the way, she turned on me. She stopped looking at me like that little girl. But she said I was a failure clinging to the past..." She turned and cast a weary look over his shoulder, and Claire ducked back. He wasn't looking at her, though; his eyes went to the spot where Leslie had been found. "She called me a loser. Pathetic... weak... I... I acted on impulse."

Overcome by emotion, Victor turned aside, shoulders heaving, and Claire's own throat constricted with pity at seeing this broken, murderous man who had loved his daughter, however terribly misguided his actions. But Tristan appeared unmoved by the display of grief.

"Doesn't matter what you *meant* to do, only what you did," Tristan uttered coldly, folding his arms across his broad chest. "And what you did got me the publicity I needed, and Leslie was the unexpected cherry on top. I'll have morbid fools flocking here for decades to see the scene of her murder. This crime remaining unsolved will only rocket the pub's stock. The only thing the people love more than tragedy is an unsolved mystery." He laughed to himself and added, "Time for you to disappear, Victor. Our business is concluded."

At that moment, Victor's weeping eyes lifted and collided directly with Claire's. She froze as their gazes locked, her breath catching in her throat. After a paralysed beat, Victor's shock shifted into blistering rage.

"*You...*" Victor snarled, dropping the money bag as his fists clenched at his sides. "Snooping around, sticking your nose where it doesn't belong."

He stepped towards Claire, murderous intent blazing in his eyes once more. Claire's instincts screamed at her to run, but she forced herself to stand firm, raising her palms.

"Now, now, let's not be hasty, old man," Tristan tutted, emerging from the shadows. His sharp eyes narrowed, gleaming like a viper sizing up prey. "So, little Miss Treadmill couldn't resist playing detective one last time. How much did you hear, hmm?"

Claire squared her shoulders, glaring back and forth between the scheming men.

"I heard everything," she stated, her voice steady despite her thundering pulse. "And I know even more. Like how *you* stole that knife, Tristan. How insanely jealous and bitter Victor was about Marco stealing his glory by attempting to break his record. How *you* manipulated that resentment, Tristan, into a murderous rage." She jabbed an accusing finger at Tristan. "This was all part of *your* ruthless plan. Have Victor eliminate your headaches and generate publicity for this place, all while lining your pockets and recouping Marco's debt."

"Good luck proving it," Tristan barked, though his composure cracked slightly.

Claire pressed her momentary advantage, stepping closer. "There's no point denying it now. The truth *is* out, and there's no squirming free this time. The police are looking for you. *Both* of you." She swivelled her glare to Victor. "Give it up. You murdered Marco. You murdered your daughter right where we stand right now. She just wanted to make you proud…"

"I never meant…"

"She knows *everything*," Tristan whispered, snatching one of the loose red bricks from the wall. He turned it over in his hand before tossing it to Victor as red sparks showed behind him. "One more for the road, old man, and there's another duffel bag in it for you."

Victor considered the brick for a moment before he started to advance on Claire. She tried to step back, to scream out, but she remained as frozen as the twisted grin lighting up Tristan's face. Just as Victor reared back to strike, a dark blur shot from the back of the pub, clutching a frying pan high. Claire heard the thud as Victor's eyes rolled back into his head. He let go of the brick and dropped to the ground to reveal Grant holding the frying pan high as he panted for breath.

"Don't move an inch," the head chef said, turning to Tristan with the frying pan, "unless you want to get whacked next, too?"

"Grant, I…" Tristan laughed, backing down the alley. "There's been a *misunderstanding*. Victor's *insane*, he…" Scrambling, Tristan leaned up against the wall. "I *gave* you the head chef job, Grant. Let's talk about it. There are two duffel bags of money right there. Pick them up and forget you saw anything."

For a split second, Grant glanced down at the bulging duffel bags of cash spilt across the ground. He lowered the frying pan and nudged open the back door of the pub. Claire's heart sank, thinking he might disappear inside and leave Tristan's crimes unpunished.

But then Grant looked back at her and Victor's unconscious form. "I heard every word they said. I called the police right before I knocked him out. There's no way they're getting away with this."

Detective Inspector Ramsbottom came thundering out of the kitchen, flanked by two uniformed officers, who swiftly apprehended Victor. As they wrestled him away, Claire found her voice again.

"Arrest Tristan as well," Claire called out urgently, pointing at Tristan's stunned figure still frozen by the pub's rear door. "He's behind all of this. I caught them discussing it. He *did* pay Victor to murder Marco for publicity. Leslie was Victor's choice… but Tristan was happy to pay for that anyway."

Ramsbottom shouted orders while the officers dragged a dazed Victor to the waiting police car. Grant maintained a safe distance, the frying pan still clutched in his hands. Tristan seized the momentary distraction to lunge for the bags of cash. Before he could reach them, Ramsbottom's booming voice cut through the commotion.

"Don't even think about it, Raybourn! You're not going anywhere."

Two more officers emerged to restrain a protesting Tristan. Claire slowly released the breath she'd been holding. It was over. Victor and Tristan would face justice for the lives they'd taken and the turmoil they'd brought down upon the village.

Claire turned to Grant, who still looked rattled, but managed a shaky smile. "Thank you. Your timing was perfect. I owe you."

He nodded. "Don't mention it. I'd say we're even."

After giving her full statement to Ramsbottom, Claire made her way back to the village square, feeling both emotionally and physically drained. She approached the crowded square and spotted Ryan and the kids amongst the revellers. They were chatting animatedly, faces smeared with ice cream as they played with sparklers. The sight filled Claire with relief and joy.

Ryan handed her a double scoop of chocolate chip as she reached them. "Couldn't resist getting one for you, too. Where'd you run off to?"

"I'll tell you... *next year*," Claire replied with a knowing smile, licking her cone.

In the distance, the flashing lights of police cars transporting Victor and Tristan away flickered and then disappeared. A weight lifted from Claire's shoulders at seeing justice finally served.

Amelia and Hugo bubbled with excitement as the midnight hour drew closer, chatting about all the fun activities and adventures they hoped to experience in the coming year. Their youthful enthusiasm was contagious.

"What's your New Year's resolution, Claire?" Hugo asked. "Mine's to finish Mario to one hundred percent."

"And I'm going to become a famous artist," Amelia said.

Claire gazed at Ryan, who slipped his arm around her waist. "My resolution is you, me, the kids... and a house to call our own. What do you say?"

"Funny, that's the exact same resolution I had in mind."

Claire tucked herself against Ryan's side, his solid warmth warding off the winter chill. Together, they watched Amelia and Hugo dance around, waving their sparklers enthusiastically.

As midnight neared, the energy in the crowd swelled. Voices shouted the countdown in unison. Claire joined in, caught up in the swelling momentum. At the stroke of twelve, with the deafening peal of the church bells and a dazzling eruption of fireworks overhead, Amelia and Hugo cheered at the top of their lungs, *"Happy New Year!"*

Laughing, Claire hugged them both tightly. Then she turned and kissed Ryan deeply. "Happy New Year. I can't wait to embark on this next chapter."

Ryan squeezed her hand, his handsome face glowing in the colourful lights. "Together. Partners till the end."

After everything they'd weathered, Claire had never felt more hopeful about the promise of new beginnings. The future shone brightly with possibility.

CHAPTER TWENTY-ONE

On New Year's Day, it was surreal to stand in The Park Inn's kitchen as a welcomed guest. At the stove, Grant stood over a sizzling pan of eggs, spatula in hand. He glanced up, offering a tentative smile that lit his normally stern features.

"Who'd have thought it was that snake Tristan all along," Grant said, "pulling old Victor's strings. I always knew he was ruthless, but to pay Victor off, murder was a step further than I'd ever have expected from him."

"I still can hardly believe it myself," Claire admitted, resting her elbows on the gleaming countertop. "Though something tells me Victor didn't need much encouragement to do what he did. Tristan might have been the one to steal that knife, but Victor's resentment was bubbling over without anyone nudging him."

She looked back over the twists and turns of the past week with its false assumptions, botched interrogations, and her repeated failure to pin down the elusive murderer. And yet, ultimately, through a combination of persistence, support, and sheer luck, the tangled threads had come together to reveal the truth.

"Suppose I should thank you for clearing my good name as well," Grant said, tipping his head to her. "Even if your methods were a bit... *aggressive*."

Claire laughed, the sting of their last confrontation still fresh. "My only excuse is I felt so sure you were hiding something."

Grant dismissed her apology with a wave of his spatula. "Water under the bridge, eh? Snooping isn't all bad. I might have never overheard anything through the back door last night if I hadn't been eavesdropping."

They shared a laugh, the awkward tension dissipating. Just then, Elena breezed into the kitchen, hugging two mugs of coffee. With her flowing embroidered dress and the sparkle returned to her eyes, she reminded Claire of a woodland sprite roaming free once more now that the shadows over Northash had passed.

Setting the mugs on the counter, Elena greeted Claire with a serene smile. "I feel as if a weight has been lifted. Victor and Tristan are behind bars." Her smile faltered slightly. "I only wish Marco and Leslie could have seen justice served as well, but I'm sure they're watching down from wherever they are."

Claire covered Elena's hand with her own, a lump forming in her throat. "Hopefully, they can both rest easier now. So…" She darted her eyes between them as Elena and Grant stood close. "Forgive me for jumping to conclusions again, but it seems you two have managed to patch things up?" When they exchanged soft smiles, her own grin widened. "I'm so very happy for you both. Truly."

Grant shrugged, a touch of pink tinging his sharp cheekbones. "We've agreed to give it another go. Figured with Marco out of the picture for good, we owed it to ourselves to try again without his interfering ways." He slid an arm around Elena's slender waist. "Maybe we can finally get things back to how they used to be before I let my jealousy mess everything up."

As Elena gazed up at Grant, Claire felt a swell of hope for the couple to blossom within. Their fractured relationship reminded her of the misunderstandings she and Ryan had navigated as stubborn youths before finally finding their way together. She offered a silent prayer that Grant and Elena's path forward into the new year would be smooth and untroubled now that the storms had passed.

"Open communication and forgiveness for past

mistakes is the only way forward," Claire offered. "And believing in each other goes a long way, too."

Elena worried her lip. "Great advice. Marco was... a blip."

"And I ought to have been more upfront with the bloke about feeling robbed of credit rather than letting it fester," Grant said, sliding the eggs onto a plate before tapping the service bell. "Could've handled things better myself, and now there's a whole load of things that will always go unsaid."

Claire lingered a moment, drinking in the comfortable domesticity between them, a vision of what might have been had Marco not interfered. With him gone and the truth exposed, she hoped Grant and Elena could now nourish the love still simmering between them into something beautiful once more.

The aroma of warming brandy and fruit suddenly filled Claire's nose, making her stomach rumble. Grant turned, lifting a silver cloche with a flourish. In the centre of a platter sat a miniature—or rather, ordinary-sized—shiny plum pudding. The very sight made Claire's mouth water as he set it on fire with a match.

"Had a trial run making Victor's original plum pudding recipe," Grant explained, setting the flaming pudding between them. "Thought it was time to see what all the fuss was about." After the flame died down, he cut out three slices and added what smelt like brandy sauce. *"Bon appétit."*

The decadent, fruity aroma embraced Claire as she accepted the plate. The pudding tasted every bit as heavenly as it appeared, infused with the richness of brandy and brown sugar, the tartness of plums tempered by sweetness. It tasted exactly like the scent of her candle, and she could see how such a creation had defined the course of several lives in their little village.

"Not worth killing over, but delicious," Claire said.

"Thinking of adding it to the menu," Grant said, tracing the plate with his fork. "Tristan was right about the morbid curiosity being great for business. After last night's arrests, we're booked up till March. Tourists are going to come whether I like it or not, so I might as well have a guaranteed best-seller on the menu. The brewery has made me the official head chef. They want me here permanently to overhaul the place, bring in a more *ethical* business model." His smile turned sheepish. "And I've persuaded them to take on Elena as my sous-chef."

"Not quite my destiny," Elena said, hugging his arm, "but I've learned a thing or two watching this one cook over the years. Our new adventure... together..."

Claire lifted her empty plate in an impromptu toast. "Well, congratulations to you both! I've no doubt you'll guide this old place into a glorious new golden era together. It's about time The Park Inn had some stability."

As she helped herself to more pudding, Claire felt a profound sense of peace settling over the 'other' pub. With justice served, redemption underway, and new love kindling from lingering embers, it seemed that, like the mythical phoenix, The Park Inn—and Northash—could rise renewed from the ashes of the tragedy that had nearly torn its community's fabric apart.

Bidding her farewells soon after with a box filled with wrapped-up plum pudding slices, Claire stepped back out into the sleepy village square with its dusting of fresh snow. Inhaling crisp, cold air scented faintly of wood smoke, she turned towards her candle shop, bathed in pale winter light. It waited to welcome her into the comforting embrace of her ordinary world—a world transformed by all she now knew it could weather and overcome.

She found Damon restocking the shelves with what was left of their basic back-ups—vanilla, cherry, coconut, rose petals, fresh linen, toffee apple—nodding his head in greeting.

"How did it go at the pub? Accuse anyone else of murder?"

"Not quite," she said with a wink. "My sleuthing days are at an end."

"For now." He fired the wink back. "I still can't believe Tristan was pulling Victor's strings. I was starting to think it had to be aliens."

Laughing, Claire sank behind the counter with a content sigh, letting the normality of the day wash over her.

"Gotta say, after everything you endured chasing the truth this past week, I'm thrilled you solved it and still made it to the other side in one piece." His eyes took on a mischievous gleam. "Does mean I owe your gran a tenner, though, since I bet this would drag past New Year's."

"You placed bets on my sleuthing success?" Claire arched a disbelieving brow, torn between irritation and amusement.

"All in good fun." Damon held up placating hands. "We knew you'd unravel it all, eventually. And now you can get back to the shop full-time. I know you've missed my hilarious daily commentary."

Claire rolled her eyes. "I am grateful for you covering while I went on my wild plum chase. Couldn't have done it without you, mate."

Damon waved her aside, but his grin held genuine warmth. "Think I speak for us all when I say we've got your back, Claire. Through triumph and tribulation alike. Nobody can hold a candle to you."

Heart swelling with affection, Claire pulled Damon into a fierce sideways hug.

The ordinary rhythm of her cherished candle shop cocooned Claire in its familiar embrace once more as customers filled the place, and before long, she had most of her favourite people crowded around the counter, sharing in Grant's delectable plum pudding.

"Utter perfection! Old Victor himself couldn't have done better." Greta dabbed her lips, eyeing another slice. "Might even be better."

Ramsbottom made a noise of agreement through a mouthful of pudding and cream. "I'll have to pass my compliments onto the chef, though I'll give him a while. He's seen my face too often, as of late."

"And mine," Claire said, toasting her fork.

"Well done, little one," Alan said, toasting his fork in return. "You *plum*bed for peace, and you achieved it."

"Oh, dear," Janet muttered. "But you're right, Greta. This might be better than Victor's. Rather morish."

Ramsbottom thumped the counter enthusiastically. "Here, here! But your father is right, Claire. You'd make a fine detective."

"You'll stick to your candle shop, though, won't you?" Janet asked eagerly. "Never seen your shelves so bare. You're welcome for the banner."

"Thank you, Mother. And I'm happy to hang up my detective hat for now."

"No greater joy than uncovering the truth, little one." Alan patted her hand. "But as fun as a complex case can be, there's a simple joy in an ending, isn't there?"

"You can say that again." Ramsbottom set down his

fork, glancing between Alan and Claire. "I'll admit, my team and I certainly botched the initial handling of everything. Victor might have slipped away with Tristan's bags of cash if Claire hadn't been so eagle-eyed."

"This investigation would have been *nothing* without my Claire," Greta said firmly after swallowing her last mouthful. "What have you learned from all of this, love?"

Claire gazed into the distance and thought of Marco and Leslie's fatal ambition, Victor's ruinous jealousy, and Tristan's ruthless scheming masked by professionalism. Her disastrous misfires and hard-learned lessons about truth's elusive nature.

"Resentments can fester if left unattended," she began slowly. "And the dangers of jumping to conclusions without examining every angle. I misjudged nearly everyone at some stage."

Ramsbottom nodded his agreement. "And I've learned not to dismiss apparent trivialities that may hold key insights." He puffed out his chest, toupee quivering. "No more cutting corners. If I'd had that recipe examined sooner, I might have uncovered the sabotage and remanded Victor before he almost escaped."

"And my takeaway," Greta announced, "is to *never* underestimate a Harris woman! That Victor never stood a chance with my Claire on the case. Never doubted you for a second."

Laughter rippled around the room at Greta's

proclamation. As it faded, Sally burst into the candle shop, windblown and distraught, dragging his suitcases behind her. Damon emerged from the stockroom as though he could sense her, and the pair reunited by the empty star candle display.

"What a *nightmare!*" Sally cried, dumping her cases. "Mum had to have her hip replaced in The Alps. Almost went headfirst over a cliff." She swiped stray hairs from her cheek with a groan. "You're lucky you stayed here, Damon. Could have been you."

Damon pulled Sally close, gently smoothing her dishevelled locks. "I was devastated I couldn't come… I…" He glanced at Claire as she cleared her throat. "Actually, I never wanted to go skiing in the first place. Don't hate me."

"You didn't?" Sally frowned at him before exhaling. "Well, you had the right idea. So, what did I miss here? Did anything interesting happen here in the weird week between Christmas and New Year? Barely had a signal all week."

"Oh, the usual," Claire said, holding back a grin. "A *few* strange things, but nothing worth mentioning."

"Well, after the week from *hell*, I don't think I'll be running away to ski any time soon," Sally announced, helping herself to some of the leftover plum pudding on the counter. "I'm ready for an actual holiday. I know that much. Given any thought to that couples' holiday?"

"Been busy with the sale," Damon announced. "How about a staycation somewhere? The Lakes, or—"

"The *Cotswolds!*" Greta interrupted, patting her pocket for her diary. "Spring... I'm off to the Cotswolds with Eugene and Marley. There's a little bowls tournament. Northash versus this village I've never heard of. Eugene's older brother, Percy, lives there..." She licked her finger and flicked through the pages. "Ah, here it is. We'll be staying in this little B&B run by some hippie in some little village called Peridale." She slapped the diary shut. "We could all go down. Rent a bus, have a little road trip!"

"A relaxing village getaway sounds divine after everything." Sally turned hopeful eyes on Damon. "What do you say? No ski slopes, guaranteed."

Damon smiled. "I say Peridale had better get ready for us."

"Mrs Beaton's nursing home is down that way," Janet said. "You'll have to pop in. We'll stay here and watch your shop, won't we, Alan?"

"Like it's our own."

"And since you're going on holiday," Janet said through pursed lips, "it would be a great time to take advantage of that new gym membership..."

Before Claire could tell her mother she'd cancelled it already, the shop bell tinkled as Ryan entered, covered in snowflakes. His gaze landed on Claire, lighting up with an affectionate smile.

"Quite the meeting. What's the topic?"

"Little Cotswold getaway later in Spring?" Greta announced, waving her diary. "It's all sorted. And you can all get practising with your bowls. Flu season has killed off some of our best, so we're a couple of team members short."

"Cotswolds?" Ryan mulled over it.

"Only if you want to?" Claire said.

"Sounds romantic," Ryan agreed, wrapping an arm around Claire's shoulder. "And peaceful."

"And according to Eugene, we're guaranteed to win the tournament," Greta added in a whisper. "Now, I best go and get Spud out before the snow gets too wild. Leave it with me. I'll arrange everything."

"And I have to get to The Park Inn for their deep clean," Janet said. "Thanks for recommending me, Ramsbottom. Quite the new contract for the new year. Alan, are you coming?"

The shop cleared one by one until only Ryan and Claire remained. Across the counter, they shared the last piece of plum pudding, and Claire nodded at the empty Christmas card display.

"You, Mr Tyler, owe the local gallery one submission of artwork as previously wagered," she said. "I sold the very last card today, which means..."

Ryan glanced at the display, but he didn't put up a fight. "A deal's a deal. You win."

Ryan pressed his forehead to hers; no more words were needed. In the snug nest of her candle shop, Claire let her eyes drift closed. The mystery had cracked wide open at last, and together, they had tended the flickering flame through darkness, a light that would lead the way into a fantastic new year. Of this, Claire felt hopeful and sure.

Thank you for reading, and don't forget to
RATE/REVIEW!

The Claire's Candles story continues in the TENTH book when Claire and the gang are off to Peridale...

DOUBLE ESPRESSO DECEPTION
COMING APRIL 2024! PRE-ORDER NOW!

Sign up to Agatha's mailing list at AgathaFrost.com and don't miss an update...

WANT TO BE KEPT UP TO DATE WITH AGATHA FROST RELEASES? *SIGN UP THE FREE NEWSLETTER!*

www.AgathaFrost.com

You can also follow **Agatha Frost** across social media. Search 'Agatha Frost' on:

Facebook
Twitter
Goodreads
Instagram

1. Pancakes and Corpses

Other

The Agatha Frost Winter Anthology

Peridale Cafe Book 1-10

Peridale Cafe Book 11-20

Claire's Candles Book 1-3

Printed in Great Britain
by Amazon

36052018R00156